He lowered her onto the bed without breaking the kiss, and his mouth on hers was hard and hungry.

"I thought…" she gasped "…you weren't home… until tomorrow."

His lips found hers again. "I'm here now," he rasped against her.

As he carried her back toward the bed, that was all that mattered.

His hands slid around her waist as his mouth came down on hers again, and the feel of his bare chest, hard against her breasts, was enough to banish the anxiety that had leapt in her—along with every other thought in her head that wasn't concerned with the immediate need to wrap herself around him until there were no joins left and the distance of the last one hundred and forty-eight days was forgotten.

None of it was as she'd planned. There was no champagne, no sexy silk nightdress, no sense of seduction, no conversation. Just skin and hands and a need so huge she felt as if it might break her wide open.

There would be a time for talking later. Tomorrow.

This was the best way she knew of bridging the spaces between them, of telling him what she wanted him to know, of reaching him.

Award-winning author

India Grey

presents

The Fitzroy Legacy
Wedlocked to the aristocratic Fitzroy family—
where shocking secrets lead to scandalous seduction

The epic romance of Kit and Sophie begins with…
CRAVING THE FORBIDDEN
On sale December 2011

And concludes with
IN BED WITH A STRANGER
On sale January 2012

Can you wait to find out what happens…?

India Grey

IN BED WITH A STRANGER

TORONTO NEW YORK LONDON
AMSTERDAM PARIS SYDNEY HAMBURG
STOCKHOLM ATHENS TOKYO MILAN MADRID
PRAGUE WARSAW BUDAPEST AUCKLAND

Recycling programs
for this product may
not exist in your area.

ISBN-13: 978-0-373-13045-0

IN BED WITH A STRANGER

First North American Publication 2012

Copyright © 2011 by India Grey

www.Harlequin.com

Printed in U.S.A.

All about the author…
India Grey

A self-confessed romance junkie, **INDIA GREY** was just thirteen years old when she first sent off for the Harlequin writers' guidelines. She can still recall the thrill of getting the large brown envelope with its distinctive logo through the letterbox. She subsequently whiled away many a dull school day staring out the window and dreaming of the perfect hero. She kept these guidelines with her for the next ten years, tucking them carefully inside the cover of each new diary in January, and beginning every list of New Year's resolutions with the words *Start Novel.*

In the meantime she also gained a degree in English literature and language from Manchester University, and in a stroke of genius on the part of the gods of romance, met her gorgeous future husband on the very last night of their three years there. The past fifteen years have been spent blissfully buried in domesticity—and heaps of pink washing generated by three small daughters—but she has never really stopped daydreaming about romance. She's just profoundly grateful to finally have an excuse to do it legitimately!

Other titles by India Grey available in ebook:

Harlequin Presents

3033—CRAVING THE FORBIDDEN*
2997—THE SECRET SHE CAN'T HIDE
2967—THE SOCIETY WIFE

*The Fitzroy Legacy

PROLOGUE

London. March.

IT WAS just a tiny piece in the property section of one of the Sunday papers. Eating brioche spread thickly with raspberry jam in the crumpled ruins of the bed that had become their world for the last three weeks, Sophie gave a little squeal.

'Listen to this!'

> *'Unexpected Twist to Fitzroy Inheritance*
> *Following the recent death of Ralph Fitzroy, eighth Earl of Hawksworth and owner of the Alnburgh estate, it has come to light that the expected heir is not, in fact, set to inherit. Sources close to the family have confirmed that the estate, which includes Alnburgh Castle and five hundred acres of land in Northumberland as well as a sizeable slice of premium real estate in Chelsea, will pass to Jasper Fitzroy, the earl's younger son from his second marriage, rather than his older brother, Major Kit Fitzroy.'*

Putting the last bit of brioche in her mouth, she continued.

> *'Major Fitzroy, a serving member of the armed forces, was recently awarded the George Cross for*

*bravery. However, it's possible that his courage failed
him when it came to taking on Alnburgh. According
to locals, maintenance of the estate has been severely
neglected in recent years, leaving the next owner with
a heavy financial burden to bear. While Kit Fitzroy is
rumoured to have considerable personal wealth, perhaps this is one rescue mission he just doesn't want to
take on...'*

She tossed the newspaper aside and, licking jam off her
fingers, cast Kit a sideways glance from under her lashes.

'"Considerable personal wealth"?' She wriggled down beneath the covers, smiling as she kissed his shoulder. 'I like
the sound of that.'

Kit, still surfacing from the depths of the sleep he'd been
blessed with since he'd had Sophie in his bed, arched an eyebrow.

'I thought as much.' He sighed, turning over and looking
straight into her sparkling, beautiful eyes. 'You're nothing
but a shallow, cynical gold-digger.'

'You're right.' Sophie nodded seriously, pressing her lips
together to stop herself from smiling. 'To be honest, I'm really
only interested in your money, and your exceptionally gorgeous Chelsea house.' The sweeping gesture she made with
her arm took in the bedroom with its view of the garden
square outside where daffodils nodded their heads along the
iron railings. 'It's why I've decided to put up with your bor-
ing personality and frankly quite average looks. Not to mention your disappointing performance in bed—'

She broke off with a squeal as, beneath the sheets, he slid
a languid hand between her thighs.

'Sorry, what was that?' he murmured gravely.

'I said...' she gasped '...that I was only interested in your...
money.' He watched her eyes darken as he moved his hand
higher. 'I've always wanted to be a rich man's plaything.'

He propped himself up on one elbow, so he could see her better. Her hair was spilling over the pillow—a gentler red than when he'd first seen her that day on the train; the colour of horse chestnuts rather than holly berries—and her face was bare of make-up. She had never looked more beautiful.

'Not a rich man's wife?' he asked idly, leaning down to kiss the hollow above her collarbone.

'Oh, no. If we're talking marriage I'd be looking for a title as well as a fortune.' Her voice turned husky as his lips moved to the base of her throat. 'And a sizeable estate to go with it...'

He smiled, taking his time, breathing in the scent of her skin. 'OK, that's good to know. Since I'm fresh out of titles and estates there's probably no point in asking.'

He felt her stiffen, heard her little gasp of shock and excitement. 'Well, there might be some room for negotiation,' she said breathlessly. 'And I'd say that right now you're in a pretty good bargaining position...'

'Sophie Greenham,' he said gravely, 'I love you because you are beautiful and clever and honest and loyal...'

'Flattery will get you a very long way.' She sighed, closing her eyes as his fingertips trailed rapture over the quivering skin on the inside of her thighs. 'And *that* will probably do the rest...'

His chest tightened as he looked down at her. 'I love you because you think underwear is a better investment than clothes, and because you're brave and funny and sexy, and I was wondering if you'd possibly consider marrying me?'

Her eyes opened and met his. The smile that spread slowly across her face was one of pure, incredulous happiness. It felt like watching the sun rise.

'Yes,' she whispered, gazing up at him with dazed, brilliant eyes. 'Yes, please.'

'I feel it's only fair to warn you that I've been disowned by my family...'

Serene, she took his face in her hands. 'We can make our own family.'

He frowned, smoothing a strand of hair from her cheek, suddenly finding it difficult to speak for the lump of emotion in his throat. 'And I have no title, no castle and no lands to offer you.'

She laughed, pulling him down into her arms. 'Believe me, I absolutely wouldn't have it any other way…'

CHAPTER ONE

Five months later.
British Military Base, Theatre of Operations.
Thursday, 6.15 a.m.

THE sun was rising, turning the sky pink and the sand to gold. Rubbing his hand over eyes that were gritty with sand and exhaustion, Kit looked out across the desert and idly wondered if he'd be alive to watch it set again.

He'd slept for perhaps an hour, maybe two, and dreamed of Sophie. Waking in the dark, his body was taut with thwarted desire, his mind racing, and the scent of her skin was still in his nostrils.

He almost preferred the insomnia.

Five months. Twenty-two weeks. One hundred and fifty-four days. By now the craving for her should have faded, but if anything it had got more intense, more impossible to ignore. He hadn't phoned her, even though at times the longing to hear her voice burned like a laser inside him, knowing that if he did it would only add fuel to the fire. And knowing that there was nothing that could be said across six thousand miles that would possibly be enough.

Just one more day.

In twenty-four hours he would be flying out of here. Flying home. There was a sense of suppressed excitement amongst the men in his unit, a mixture of relief and exhilaration that had been building over the last week as the days dwindled.

It was a feeling Kit didn't share.

He'd been in bomb disposal for a long time. He'd never thought of it as anything other than a job; a dirty, awkward, challenging, exhausting, addictive, necessary job. But that was in the days when he thought rather than felt. When his emotions had been comfortably locked away in some part of him that was buried so deep he didn't even know it was there.

Everything was different now. He wasn't who he'd thought he was—quite literally thanks to the lies the man he'd called his father had told him all his life. But also, loving Sophie had blown him wide open, revealing parts of him he hadn't known existed, and now the job seemed dirtier, the stakes higher, the odds shorter. So much shorter.

One more day. Would his luck last?

'Major Fitzroy—coffee, sir. We're almost ready to move out.'

Kit turned. Sapper Lewis had emerged from the mess hut and was walking towards him, spilling most of the coffee. An earnest kid of nineteen, he had the gawky enthusiasm of a Great Dane puppy. It made Kit feel about a thousand years old. He took the enamel mug and grimaced as he swallowed.

'Thank you, Lewis,' Kit drawled. 'Other men I know have curvaceous secretaries to bring them coffee in the morning. I have you to bring me something that tastes like freshly brewed dirt.'

Lewis grinned. 'You'll miss me when you get home.'

'I sincerely doubt it.' Kit took another mouthful of coffee and chucked the rest into the dust as he began to walk away. Not before he'd seen Lewis's face fall though.

'Fortunately you make a far better infantryman than a barista,' he called back over his shoulder. 'Bear that in mind when you get home, won't you?'

'Yes, sir!' Lewis hurried after him. 'And can I just say

how great it's been working with you, sir? I've learned loads. Before this tour I wasn't sure I wanted to stay in the army, but watching you has made me decide to go into EOD.'

Kit stopped. Rubbing a hand across his jaw, he turned round.

'Do you have a girlfriend, Sapper?'

Lewis shifted from foot to foot, his face a mixture of pride and embarrassment. His Adam's apple bobbed. 'Yeah. Kelly. She's expecting a baby in two months' time. I'm going to ask her to marry me this leave.'

Narrowing his eyes as he looked out to the flat horizon, Kit nodded.

'You love her?'

'Yes, sir.' He scuffed the dust with the toe of his boot. 'We haven't been together long, but…yeah. I really love her.'

'Then take my advice. Learn to make a decent coffee and get yourself a job in Starbucks after all, because love and bomb disposal don't mix.' With a cool smile Kit handed the enamel mug back to him. 'Now, let's get out there and get this done so we can all go home.'

'Sorry I'm late.'

Smiling broadly in a way that didn't remotely suggest contrition and trying not to knock over anyone's designer beer with her shopping bags, Sophie slid into the chair opposite Jasper at the little metal table.

He eyed the bags archly. 'I take it you were unavoidably detained in…' His brows shot up another inch as he saw the discreet logo of Covent Garden's 'erotic boutique' on the corner of the biggest bag. 'Kit's in for a treat when he gets home.'

Shoving the bags under the table, Sophie tucked the great big bunch of vibrantly coloured flowers she'd just bought into the empty chair beside her and tried to stop herself from grinning like a love-struck loon.

'I've just spent an indecent amount of money,' she admitted, snatching up a menu and sliding her sunglasses onto the top of her head to read it. The table Jasper had chosen was in the shade of a red awning, which gave a healthy glow to his poetic pallor. He was so different from Kit it was incredible that they'd believed they were brothers for so long.

'On some pretty indecent stuff, if I know that shop.' Jasper peered into a corner of the bag.

'It's just a nightdress thing,' Sophie said hastily, hoping he wouldn't take out the wicked little slip of silvery-grey silk and display it in front of the lunch crowd outside Covent Garden's busiest restaurant. 'I was passing, and as I just got paid for the vampire movie, and Kit is coming home tomorrow I thought, What the hell? But really, it was way too expensive.'

'Don't be daft. Your days of buying clothes from charity shops and bread from the reduced shelf in the supermarket are over now, darling.' Jasper looked around to catch the eye of the waiter, then turned back to her and rubbed his hands together as if in anticipation. 'Just a few hours left of single-girldom before Kits gets home and you become a full-time fiancée. Planning any wild parties?'

'I'm saving that for when he gets back, in about…' Sophie checked the time on her phone '…twenty-eight hours. Let's see…they're five hours ahead of us, so he should be just finishing his last shift about now.'

Jasper must have caught the note of anxiety in her voice because he covered her hand with his. 'Don't think about it,' he said firmly. 'You've done brilliantly—I'd have gone out of my mind with worry if it had been Sergio out there, dicing with death every day. You're very brave.'

'Hardly, compared to Kit.' Her throat dried and she looked down at the menu as the waiter made his way towards them. She tried to picture Kit now—hot, dirty, exhausted. For five months he had been looking after a battalion of men, putting their needs above his own. She wanted him home so she could look after him.

Amongst other things.

'Soph?'

'What? Oh, sorry.' Realising the waiter's pen was poised for her to give her order, Sophie asked for a Salade Niçoise, which was the first thing that caught her eye. Scribbling it down, the waiter moved away, his slim hips swaying as he wove through the tables.

'Kit's used to it,' Jasper said absently, watching him go. 'He's been doing it for years. How is he, anyway?'

'Oh…you know…he sounds OK,' she lied vaguely. 'But I want to hear about you. Are you and Sergio all packed and ready to hit tinseltown?'

Jasper leaned back in his chair and rubbed his hands over his face. 'The packing's ongoing, but, believe me, I have never been more ready for anything in my life. After everything that's happened in the last six months—Dad dying, the whole coming-out thing, Alnburgh turning out to be mine and not Kit's—I can't wait to get on that plane and just leave it all behind. I intend to spend the next three months lying by the pool drinking cocktails while Sergio's at work.'

'If I didn't know you better I'd say you were ruthlessly attempting to make me wild with envy.'

'Rumbled.' Jasper grinned as the waiter arrived, his tray held high. 'Is it working?'

'Nope.' The waiter placed a large gin and tonic clinking with ice in front of her. 'The pool and the cocktails sound lovely, but honestly for the first time in my life I have no desire to be anywhere other than here. Well, not *here*, obviously,' she said, nodding towards one of Covent Garden's famous street performers, 'since there's only so long I could watch a poncey out-of-work actor juggle with knives. But at home. With Kit.'

Jasper eyed her narrowly, tapping his pursed lips thoughtfully with a finger.

'I'm thinking alien abduction. I know there should be a more logical explanation for this complete character transformation from the girl who still has a phone on pay-as-you-go because a contract is too much commitment, to the woman whose idea of excitement is…' he waved a dismissive hand '…pegging out washing or something, but I just can't think what it could be…'

'Love,' Sophie said simply, taking a mouthful of gin. 'And maybe, having been on the move constantly all my life, I'm just ready to stay still now.' She glanced at him guiltily. 'I keep sneaking into furniture shops to look at sofas and I've developed a terrible obsession with paint colour charts. I suppose I just want a home.'

'Well, Kit's pad in one of Chelsea's most desirable garden squares isn't a bad start on the property ladder,' Jasper said, scooping up crab pâté on a piece of rye bread. 'Better than Alnburgh, anyway. You had a narrow escape there.'

'You can say that again. So, are you planning to move in when you get back from LA, then?'

Jasper grimaced. 'God, no. The windswept Northumberland coast is hardly the hub of the film industry and I can't exactly see Sergio walking down to the village shop and asking Mrs Watts for foie gras and the latest copy of *Empire* magazine.'

Taking another mouthful of gin, Sophie hid a smile. He was right; Sergio had shown up in Alnburgh for Ralph's funeral and it had been like seeing a parrot at the North Pole.

'So what will happen to it?' She speared an olive from her salad. Curiously, she cared much more about the future of Alnburgh Castle now there was no question of it involving Kit or her. She'd been so miserable there when she'd gone up to stay with Jasper last winter that the thought of actually living within its cold stone walls was enough to bring her out in goosebumps. But now that possibility had been removed, and sitting in the sunshine in the middle of Covent Garden, she could feel a sort of abstract affection for the place.

'I don't know.' Jasper sighed again. 'The legal situation is utterly incomprehensible and the finances are worse. It's such a bloody mess—I still can't forgive Dad for dropping a bomb-shell like that in his will. The fact that Kit isn't his natural son is just a technicality—he was brought up at Alnburgh and he's taken responsibility for the place almost single-handed for the last fifteen years. I guess that if I'm gutted by the way things have turned out, it must be even worse for him. Has he mentioned it in his letters or anything?'

Not meeting his eye, Sophie shook her head.

'No, he hasn't mentioned it.'

The fact was he hadn't mentioned anything much. Before he went he'd warned her that phone calls were frustrating and best avoided so she hadn't expected him to ring, but she couldn't help being a bit disappointed that he hadn't. She had written to him several times a week—long letters, full of news and silly anecdotes and how much she was missing him. His replies had been infrequent, short and impersonal, and had left her feeling more lonely than if he hadn't written at all.

'I just hope he doesn't hate me too much, that's all,' Jasper said unhappily. 'Alnburgh meant everything to him.'

'Don't be silly. It's not your fault that Kit's mother disap-peared with another man when he was just a little boy, is it? And anyway, it's all in the past now, and, as my barking-mad mother would say, everything happens for a reason. If Kit was the heir there'd be absolutely no chance I'd be marrying him. He'd need a horsey wife who came complete with her own heirloom tiara and a three-year guarantee to produce a son. I'd fail on all counts.'

Her tone was flippant, but her smile stiffened slightly as she said the bit about the son. Jasper didn't seem to notice.

'You come closer than Sergio. You'd both look good in a

tiara, but you certainly have the edge when it comes to bearing heirs.'

'I wouldn't bet on it.'

It was no good. To her shame both her voice and her smile cracked and she had to press her hand to her mouth. Across the table Jasper looked horrified.

'Soph? What's wrong?'

She grabbed her drink and took a gulp. The gin was cold, bitter, good. It felt as if it was clearing her head, although that was probably an ironic illusion.

'I'm fine. I finally saw a doctor about the monthly hell that is my period, that's all.'

Jasper's eyes widened. 'God, Soph—it's nothing—?'

She waved a hand. 'No, no, nothing serious. It's as I thought—endometriosis. The good news is it's not life-threatening, but the bad news is that there's not much they can do about it and it could make getting pregnant a problem.'

'Oh, honey. I had no idea having children was so important to you.'

'Neither did I, until I met Kit.' Sophie slid her sunglasses back down, feeling in need of something to hide behind. Having spent years listening to her mother and the women in the haphazard commune in which she'd grown up analyse everything in minute, head-wrecking detail, she usually went out of her way to avoid any kind of serious discussion, but there was part of her that wanted to share this bittersweet new feeling. 'Finding out it might be difficult has made me realise how important it is—how's that for irony?' She sighed. 'Anyway, the doctor didn't say it was impossible, just that it could take a long time and it was best not to leave it too long.'

He reached across the table and took her hand.

'So when are you going to start trying?'

Sophie looked at her phone again and looked up at him with a determined smile. 'In about twenty-seven and a half hours.'

* * *

The second hand quivered slightly as it edged wearily around the clock face. Sitting on a plastic chair in Intensive Care, watching it with wide-eyed fatigue, Kit kept thinking that it wouldn't make it through the next minute.

He knew the feeling.

He had been here since late afternoon, English time, when the emergency medical helicopter had finally landed, bringing Sapper Kyle Lewis home. Sedated into unconsciousness, with bullets in his head and chest, it wasn't quite the homecoming Lewis had looked forward to.

Kit sank his head into his hands. The now familiar, tingling numbness was back, stealing up through his fingertips until he felt as if he were dissolving.

'Coffee, Major Fitzroy?'

He jerked upright again. The nurse in front of him wore a blue plastic disposable apron and was smiling kindly, unaware of the stab of anguish her question caused. He looked away, his teeth gritted.

'No, thanks.'

'Can I get you anything for the pain?'

He turned, eyes narrowed. Did she know that *he* was the reason Lewis was in the room behind him, hooked up to machines that were breathing for him as his mother held his hand and wept softly, and the girlfriend he had spoken of so proudly kept her terrified eyes averted?

'Your face,' the nurse said gently. 'I know you were seen to in the field hospital, but the medication they gave you will have worn off now.' She tilted her head, looking at him with great compassion. 'They might only be superficial, but these shrapnel wounds can be very painful as they heal.'

'It looks worse than it is.' He'd seen his face in the washroom mirror and felt dull surprise at the torn flesh and bruising around his eyes. 'Nothing that a large whisky wouldn't fix.'

The nurse smiled. 'I'm afraid I can't give you one of those here. But you could go home now, you know.' The plastic apron crackled as she moved past him to the door of Lewis's room, pausing with her hand on the doorplate. 'His family's here now. You've looked after these boys for five months, Major,' she said gently. 'It's time you looked after yourself.'

Kit got a brief glimpse of the inert figure in the bed before the door swung shut again. He exhaled heavily, guilt squeezing the air from his lungs.

Home.

Sophie.

The thought of her almost severed the last shreds of his self-control. He looked at the clock again, realising that although he'd been staring at it for hours he had no idea what time it was.

Almost six o'clock in the evening, and he was almost three hundred miles away. He stumbled to his feet, his mind racing, his heart suddenly beating hard with the need to get to her. To feel her in his arms and lose himself in her sweetness and forget...

Behind him a door opened, pulling him back into the present. Turning he saw Lewis's girlfriend come out of the room, her thin shoulders hunched, her pregnant stomach incongruously out of proportion with the rest of her. Slumping against the wall, she looked appallingly young.

'They won't say anything. I just want to know if he's going to be OK.' She spoke with a kind of sulky defiance, but Kit could see the fear in her face when she looked at him. 'Is he?'

'Wing Commander Randall's the army medic here. According to him, he's over the worst now,' Kit said tersely. 'If soldiers survive the airlift to the camp hospital their chances of survival are already ninety-seven percent. He's made it all the way home.'

Her scowl deepened. 'I don't mean is he going to survive. I mean is he going to be OK? I mean, back to normal. Because I don't think I could stand it if he wasn't...' She broke off, turning her face away. Kit could see her throat working frantically as she swallowed back tears. 'We don't even know each other that well,' she went on, after a moment. 'We'd not been going out long when *this* happened.' A sharp gesture of her head told him she was referring to the pregnancy. 'It wasn't exactly planned but, as my mum says, it was my own fault. Just got to get on with it now.' She looked at Kit with dead eyes then; inky tears were running down her face. 'And what about this? If he's…I dunno…*injured*, I'm stuck with it, aren't I? But whose fault is that?'

Mine, Kit wanted to say. *All mine.*

What right did he have to forget that?

Sophie's eyes snapped open.

She lay very still, staring into the soft summer darkness, all her senses on high alert as she listened out for a repeat of the sound that had woken her.

Or maybe it hadn't even been a sound. Maybe it was just a feeling. A dream perhaps? Or an instinct…

She sat up, struggling from sleep, the hairs rising on the back of her neck. The blood was swishing in her ears, but outside she could hear the usual sounds of the city at night— traffic on the King's Road, a distant siren, a car moving through the square below.

And then something else, closer, inside the house. A muffled thud, like something being dropped, followed by the soft, heavy tread of someone coming slowly up the stairs.

Sophie froze.

Then, with a muttered curse, she kicked off the covers and scrambled to her feet on the bed, looking frantically around for a weapon and finding herself fervently wishing she'd taken up cricket or baseball. Her heart was galloping. It was no good—there was nothing remotely suited to fending off an intruder within reach, and she realised that she should simply have rolled off the bed and hidden underneath it…

A shape appeared in the doorway, filling it, just as Sophie's pounding heart seemed to have filled her throat. It was too late to move now, too late to do anything but brazen it out.

'Don't move,' she croaked. 'I have a weapon.'

With what sounded like a sigh the intruder took a step forwards.

'Where I've just come from we don't call that a weapon. We call that a TV remote.'

His voice was hoarse with fatigue, sexy as hell and instantly familiar.

'Kit!'

It was a cross between a shout of jubilation and a sob. In a split second Sophie had bounded across the bed and he caught her as she hurtled into his arms, wrapping her legs tightly around his waist as their mouths met. Questions half formed themselves in her brain, bubbling up then dissolving again in the more urgent need to feel him and touch him and keep on kissing him…

He lowered her onto the bed without breaking the kiss, and his mouth on hers was hard and hungry. Sliding her hands into his hair, she felt grit. He smelled of earth and antiseptic, but beneath that she caught the scent that made her senses reel—the dry cedar-scent that was all his own, that she had craved like a drug.

'I thought…' she gasped '…you weren't home…until tomorrow.'

His lips found hers again.

'I'm here now,' he rasped against her.

Now that they were both together on the bed, that was all that mattered.

Desire gushed through her, slippery and quick. Laying her down on the bed, he straightened up, towering over her for a second. Shadows obscured his face, but in spite of the darkness she caught the silvery glitter of his eyes and it sent another wave of urgent need crashing through her. Rising up onto her knees, she pulled off her T-shirt, stopping with her mouth the low moan he uttered as her naked body moved against him.

'Are you all right?' she murmured moments later, fumbling for the buttons on his shirt with shaking fingers.

'Yes.'

It was a primitive growl that came from low in his chest. He pulled away, half turning as he yanked his shirt from his trousers and wrenched it over his head. In that moment the light from the street filtering through a gap in the curtains caught his face and Sophie gasped.

'No—you're hurt. Kit, your face—'

She got to her feet, reaching for him, taking his face between her hands and stroking her thumbs with great tenderness over the lacerations on his cheekbones until she felt him flinch away.

'It's nothing.'

His hands slid around her waist as his mouth came down on hers again, and the feel of his bare chest, hard against her breasts, was enough to banish the anxiety that had leapt in her, along with every other thought in her head that wasn't concerned with the immediate need to wrap herself around him. To feel him against her and inside her until there were no joins left and the distance of the last one hundred and fifty-four days was forgotten.

His hands were warm on her back, moving across her quivering skin with a certainty and steadiness of touch she couldn't possibly match as she struggled to undo his belt, impatient to get rid of the last barriers that stood between them. She gave a gasp of triumph as she managed to work the buttons free. Swiftly he kicked off his desert combats and they fell back onto the bed.

None of it was as she'd planned. There was no champagne, no sexy silk nightdress, no sense of seduction, no conversation, just skin and hands and a need so huge she felt as if it might break her wide open.

There would be a time for talking. Later. Tomorrow.

This was the best way she knew of bridging the spaces between them, of telling him what she wanted him to know, of reaching him. Just like the first time they'd made love, on the night he'd found out that Ralph Fitzroy wasn't his father. There had been nothing she could say then because it was too big, too raw, too complex, but for a while it had been flamed into insignificance in the heat of their passion.

His body was rigid with tension, his shoulders like concrete beneath her fingers. They were both shaking, but as he entered her she felt some of the tightness leave his body as if he too felt the wild, exhilarating rightness that surged through her. Her arms were locked around his neck, their foreheads touching, and the feel of his breath on her cheek, his skin, was almost enough to make her come. Her body shivered and burned, but fiercely she held back, tightening her muscles around him, holding on like a woman in danger of drowning.

With a moan he slid his arms beneath her back, gathering her up and pulling her hard against his chest as he sat up. Sophie wrapped her legs around his waist, and the increase in pressure was enough to tip her over the edge. She let go, arching backwards and gasping as her orgasm ripped through her.

He held her, waiting until it had subsided before pulling her back into his arms and burying his face in her neck. She could feel him inside her still, and slowly she rotated her pelvis, stroking his hair, holding him tightly until he stiffened and cried out her name.

Together they collapsed back onto the bed. Cradling his head against her breasts, Sophie stared up into the darkness and smiled.

CHAPTER TWO

KIT woke suddenly, his body convulsing with panic.

It took a few seconds for reality to reassert itself. It was light—the cool, bluish light of an English morning, and the sheets were clean and smooth against his skin. Sophie was lying on her side, tucked into his body, one hand flat on his chest, over his frantically thudding heart.

The fact that he wasn't actually walking along a dust track towards a bridge with a bomb beneath it told him he must have slept. After a hundred and fifty-four largely sleepless nights it felt like a small miracle.

He shifted position slightly so he could look into Sophie's sleeping face, stretching limbs that had stiffened from being still for so long. His heart squeezed. God, she was so lovely. The summer had brought out a faint sprinkling of freckles over the bridge of her nose, and put a bloom into her creamy cheeks. Or maybe that was last night. The erection he'd woken up with intensified as he remembered, and he looked at her mouth. Her top lip with its steep upwards sweep and pronounced Cupid's bow was slightly swollen from his kisses.

It was also curved into the faintest and most secretive of smiles.

Deeply asleep, she looked serene and self-contained, as if she was travelling through wonderful places where he could never hope to follow, full of people he didn't know. No godforsaken, mine-strewn desert roads for her, he thought bleakly.

The light filtering through the narrow gap in the curtains gleamed on her smooth bare shoulder and cast a halo around her hair. Picking up a silken strand, he wound it lazily around his finger, thinking back to one of the last times he had lain here beside her and asked her to marry him.

What a fool. What a selfish, stupid fool.

Anything could have happened. He thought of Lewis's girlfriend; her terrified eyes and her swollen stomach. *We don't even know each other that well… If he's…injured, I'm stuck with it, aren't I?* What if it had been him instead of Lewis? They'd only had three weeks together. *Three weeks.* How could he have expected Sophie to stand by him for a lifetime when he barely knew her?

The gleaming lock of hair fell back onto her creamy shoulder, but he left his hand there, holding it in front of his face and stretching his fingers. They shook slightly, prickling with pins and needles, and he curled them into a fist, squeezing hard.

Harder.

The bones showed white beneath his sun-darkened skin and pain flared through the stretched tendons, but it didn't quite manage to drive away the numbness, or stop the slideshow that was replaying itself in his head again. The heat shimmering over the road, the hard sun glinting off windows in the buildings above. That eerie silence. The way everything had seemed to slip into slow motion, as if it were happening underwater. His hands trembling uncontrollably; the wire cutters slipping through his nerveless fingers as the voice in his earpiece grew more urgent, telling him that a sniper had been spotted…

And then the gunshots.

He sat up, swearing under his breath. Dragging a hand

over his face, he winced as he caught a scab that had begun
to form on one of the cuts across his cheekbone.

He was home, and back with Sophie. So why did it feel
as if he were still fighting, and further away from her than
ever?

Sophie stopped in the kitchen doorway.

Kit was sitting at the table with the pile of letters that had
come while he'd been away, drinking coffee. He was wearing jeans but no shirt, and his skin was tanned to the colour
of mahogany. Sophie's stomach flipped.

'Hi.'

Oh, dear. Having leapt out of bed almost as soon as she
opened her eyes, brushed her teeth like a person on speeded-
up film and even slapped a bit of tinted moisturiser onto her
too-pale cheeks before running downstairs, it was ridiculous
that that was all she could manage. *Hi.* And in a voice that
was barely more than a strangled whisper.

He looked up. The morning light showed up the mess of
cuts and bruising on his face, making him look battered and
exhausted and beautiful.

'Hi.'

'So you *are* real,' she said ruefully, going across to fill the
kettle. 'I thought I might have dreamed it. It wouldn't be the
first time I'd done that while you've been gone—dreamed
about you so vividly that waking up was like saying goodbye all over again.' She stopped, before she said any more
and gave herself away as being a terrifying, crazy, obsessive
fiancée. To make it sound as if she were joking she asked,
'Did they let you off a day early for good behaviour?'

'Unfortunately not.' He put down the letter he was reading and pushed a hand through his hair. It was still wet from
the shower, but she could see that it had been lightened by
the sun, giving the kind of tawny streaks only the most ex-

pensive hairdressers could produce. 'A man in my unit was badly injured yesterday. I flew home with him.'

'Oh, Kit, I'm so sorry.' Filled with contrition for thinking such shallow thoughts, Sophie went over to stand beside him. 'How is he?'

'Not good.'

His voice was flat, toneless, and he looked down at the letter again, as if the subject was closed. On the other side of the kitchen the kettle began its steam-train rattle. Sophie touched his cheekbone with her fingertips.

'What happened?' she said softly. 'Was it an explosion?'

For a moment he said nothing, but she saw his eyelids flicker, as if he was remembering something he didn't want to remember; reliving something he didn't want to relive.

'Yes…'

His forehead creased into a sudden frown of pain and for a second she thought he was going to say more. But then the shutters descended and he looked up at her with a cool smile that was more about masking emotion than conveying it.

Sophie pulled out the chair beside him and sat down, turning to face him. 'How badly hurt is he?'

'It's hard to tell at the moment,' he said neutrally. 'It looks like he'll live, but it's too early to say how bad his injuries will be.' His smile twisted. 'He's only nineteen.'

'Just a boy,' she murmured. The kettle boiled in a billow of steam and hissed into silence. Aching for him, Sophie took his hand between hers, feeling the hard skin on the undersides of his fingers, willing him to open up to her. 'It's good that you stayed with him. It must have made a huge difference to him, having you there, and to his family, knowing that someone was looking after him…'

She trailed off as he got abruptly to his feet, giving her no choice but to let go of his hand.

'Coffee?'

'Yes, please.' Hurt blossomed inside her but she didn't let it seep into her tone. 'Sorry—there's only instant. I was going to go shopping today to get things in for when you came back.'

She thought of all the plans she had made for his home-coming; the food she was going to buy that could be eaten in bed—olives, quails' eggs, tiny dim sum and Lebanese pastries from the deli around the corner—champagne and proper coffee, piles of croissants and brioche for breakfast. And the X-rated silk nightdress, of course. Now they all seemed to belong to a silly, frilly fantasy in which Kit took the part of the Disney Prince, doe-eyed with adoration.

The reality was turning out to be slightly different.

'What on earth have you been living on?' he said, his voice an acerbic drawl. 'I was going to make you breakfast, but the cupboard seems to be bare.'

'I usually eat on the go,' she said lightly, getting up and going over to the designer stainless-steel bread bin. 'But look, there's bread. And…' she opened a cupboard and pulled down a jar with a flourish '…chocolate spread.'

Splinters of guilt lodged themselves in Kit's throat. She was making a good attempt to hide it but behind the show of nonchalance he could tell she was hurt. She'd tried to reach out to him—to *talk* to him like a normal human being, and he'd behaved as if she'd done something indecent.

It must have made a huge difference to him, having you there, and to his family, knowing that someone was looking after him…

How she overestimated him. In so many ways.

He looked at her. She was putting bread into the toaster and her glossy hair was tousled, her legs long and bare beneath an old checked shirt she must have taken from his wardrobe. He felt his chest tighten with remorse and desire. He wasn't brave enough to shatter her illusions about him yet, but he could at least try to make up to her for being such a callous bastard.

Gently he took the jar from her and unscrewed the lid. He peered inside and then looked at her, raising an eyebrow.

'You actually *eat* this stuff?'

She shrugged, reaching for a knife from the cutlery drawer. 'What else would you do with it?'

'I'm surprised,' he said gravely, taking the knife from her too, 'that you need to ask that...'

Looking at her speculatively, keeping his face completely straight, he reached out and undid the buttons of her shirt. He felt her jump slightly at his touch and she let out a little sound of surprise. But as he took hold of her waist and lifted her onto the countertop her green eyes glittered with instant excitement.

Slowly, with great focus he dipped the tip of the blade into the jar, loading it with soft, velvety chocolate. The moment stretched as he turned the knife around in his hand, then turned his attention to her, moving the edge of her shirt aside to expose her bare breast.

It took considerable self-control to keep the lust that was rampaging through him from showing on his face, or in his movements. His hand shook slightly as he cupped her warm, perfect breast. Behind them, the toast sprang up in the toaster and she jumped, giving a little indrawn breath. In one smooth sweep, Kit spread the chocolate over her skin.

Abstractly, as he parted his lips to taste her, he thought how beautiful it looked—the chocolate against the vanilla cream of her skin. But then all thoughts were driven from his head as he took her chocolate-covered nipple into his mouth and felt her stiffen and arch against him.

His tongue teased her, licking her clean. The chocolate was impossibly sweet and cloying and it masked the taste of her skin, so without lifting his head he reached behind her and turned the tap on, running cold water into the cup of his hand. Straightening up, he let it trickle onto her, watching her eyes widen in shock as the cold water ran down her skin.

'Kit, you—!'

His mouth was on hers before she could finish. Sitting on the granite countertop, she was the same height as he was and he put his hands on her bottom, pulling her forwards so that her thighs were tight around his waist, her pelvis hard against his erection.

God, he loved her. He loved her straightforwardness, her generosity. He loved the way she seemed to understand him, and her willingness to give him what he needed. He didn't have to find words, not when he could show her how he felt this way.

Her arms were around his neck, her fingers tangling in his damp hair. He was just about to lift her up, hitch her around him and haul her over to the table where he could take her more easily when there was a loud knock at the front door.

He stopped, stepping backwards, cursing quietly and with more than a hint of irony, given his choice of word.

'Don't answer it.'

It was tempting, so tempting, given how utterly, outrageously sexy she looked sprawled on the kitchen countertop, her wet shirt open, her mouth bee-stung from his kisses. He dragged a hand over his face, summoning the shreds of his control.

'I have to,' he said ruefully, heading for the door. 'It's breakfast. I ordered it when you were sleeping, and since they only agreed to home delivery as a special favour...'

Left alone in the kitchen, Sophie pulled her shirt together and slid shakily down from the worktop, her trembling legs almost giving way beneath her as she tried to stand. Through the thick fog of desire she was dimly aware of voices in the hallway—one Kit's, the other vaguely familiar. Dreamily she picked up the chocolate spread and dipped her finger into it, closing her eyes and tipping her head back as she put it in her mouth.

'In here?'

The vaguely familiar voice was closer now and she jumped, opening her eyes in time to see an even more familiar face come into the kitchen; so familiar that for a moment she thought it was someone she must know from way back—a friend of Jasper's, perhaps?

'Hi. You must be Sophie.'

Grinning, the man put a wooden crate stacked with aluminium cartons on the table and held out his hand. Sophie shook it, feeling guilty that she couldn't quite place him and managing to say hello without making it obvious she couldn't remember his name.

Kit came in carrying a bottle of champagne.

'Thanks, I appreciate this.'

'No big deal—it's the least I can do considering you've spent the last five months being a hero. It's good to see you back in one piece—or nearly.'

He gestured to the shrapnel wounds on Kit's face. Sophie noticed the tiny shift in Kit's expression; the way it darkened, tightened.

'How's the restaurant?' he asked smoothly.

'Good, thanks, although I don't get to spend as much time there as I'd like, thanks to the TV stuff. I just got back from filming for a new series in the US.'

Horror congealed like cold porridge in Sophie's stomach as her eyes flew back to the man. She now realised why he was vaguely familiar. Suddenly she was aware that she was standing in the same kitchen as one of the country's top celebrity chefs wearing a wet shirt that barely skimmed her bottom and clung to her breasts, eating chocolate spread with her finger straight from the jar.

Surreptitiously she put the jar down and tried to shrink backwards behind the large vase of flowers she'd bought in Covent Garden. Luckily the Very Famous Chef was engrossed in a discussion about business with Kit as they headed back towards the door, but he did pause in the doorway and look back at her.

'Nice to meet you, Sophie. You must get Kit to bring you to the restaurant some time.'

Not on your life, thought Sophie, smiling and nodding; not now he'd seen her like this. As soon as he'd gone she picked up the jar of chocolate spread and was eating it with a spoon when Kit came back in.

'You could have warned me,' she moaned between spoonfuls.

'Sorry,' Kit drawled, 'but I was pretty distracted myself.'

'He's a friend of yours?'

'That depends on your definition of friend. I know him reasonably well because his restaurant is just around the corner from here and I've been there enough times over the years.'

Sophie took another spoonful of chocolate spread. People didn't go to restaurants on their own. She pictured the kind of women Mr Celeb-Chef must have seen with Kit in the past, and the contrast they must have made with her, now.

Kit was looking at the foil trays in the crate. 'Put down that revolting sweet stuff; we have smoked-salmon bagels, blueberry pancakes, almond croissants, proper coffee, oh—and this, of course.' He held up the bottle of champagne. 'So—do you want to eat here, or in bed?'

Sophie's resistance melted like butter in a microwave. She found that she was smiling.

'What do you think?'

Sophie walked slowly back to Kit's house, trailing her fingers along the railings outside the smart houses, a bag filled with supplies from the uber-stylish organic supermarket on the King's Road bumping against her leg. She felt she had some ground to make up after the incriminating chocolate-spread incident this morning.

The thought of chocolate spread drew her attention to the

pleasurable ache in her thighs as she walked, and she couldn't stop her mind from wandering ahead of her, to the house with the black front door at the far end of the square. From this distance it looked the same as all its expensive, exclusive neighbours, but Sophie felt a little quiver inside her at the thought that Kit was there.

She had left him going through yet more of the post that had arrived while he'd been away, and she reluctantly had to admit it had been almost a relief to have an excuse to get out of the house. They had eaten breakfast and made love, slowly and luxuriously, then lain drowsily together as the clouds moved across the clean blue sky beyond the window and the morning slid into afternoon. Then they had made love again.

It had been wonderful. More than wonderful—completely magical. So why did she have the uneasy feeling that it was a substitute for talking?

There was so much she wanted to say, and even more that she wanted him to tell her. She thought of the contraceptive pills she'd thrown in the bin and felt a hot tide of guilt that she hadn't actually got round to mentioning that. But how could she when it felt as if he had put up an emotion-proof fence around himself? There might as well be a sign above his head: 'Touch, but Don't Talk.'

She was being ridiculous, she told herself sternly, reaching into her pocket for her key. They'd spent whole days in bed before he'd gone away and gone for hours without speaking a word, lost in each other's bodies or just lying with their limbs entwined, reading. It wasn't a sign that something was wrong. If anything, surely it was the opposite?

She slid the key into the lock and opened the door.

The house was silent, but the atmosphere was different now Kit was home. There was a charge to it. An electricity, which both excited and unnerved her. Going into the sleek granite and steel kitchen, she remembered what she'd said to Jasper about wanting a home. The flowers she'd bought in such a surge of optimism and excitement stood in the centre of the black granite worktop, a splash of colour against the masculine monochrome.

She put the kettle on.

For the last five months this had been her home, around the time she'd spent in Romania filming the stupid vampire movie, but now Kit was back it suddenly seemed to be his house again, a place where she was the guest. Even her flowers looked wrong—as out of place as her low-rent white sliced bread in his designer bread bin and her instant coffee in his tasteful Conran Shop mugs.

Dispiritedly she spooned fragrant, freshly ground Fairtrade coffee into the coffee maker, hoping she'd got that right at least. Taking down a tray, she set it with mugs, and milk in a little grey jug, but then wondered if that was trying too hard? After a moment's indecision she took them off again. Pouring the coffee straight into the mugs, she picked them up and went to find Kit.

He was upstairs, in the room at the front of the house that he used as a study. Outside the half-open door she hesitated, then knocked awkwardly.

'Yes?'

'I made you some coffee.'

'Thank you.' From inside the room his voice was an amused drawl. 'Do I have to come out to collect it, or are you going to bring it in?'

'I don't want to disturb you,' she muttered, pushing the door open and going in.

The surface of the desk in front of him was covered in piles of letters, and the waste-paper bin was full of envelopes. Sophie felt a fresh wave of lust and love and shyness as she looked at him. The cuts over his cheekbones were still raw-looking, the bruising beneath his eyes still dark, making him look inexpressibly battered and weary.

'Hmm…that's a good point,' he murmured wryly, trailing his fingers up the back of her bare leg beneath the skirt of her little flowered dress as she bent to put the mug on the desk. 'You are *very* disturbing.'

Desire leapt inside her, inflaming flesh that already burned. She doused it down. Turning round, she leaned her bottom on the edge of the desk and looked at him over the rim of her mug, determined to attempt a form of communication that didn't end in orgasm for once.

'So, is there anything interesting in all that?'

Picking up his coffee, Kit shrugged, his expression closed. 'Not much. Bank statements and share reports. Some more information about the Alnburgh estate.' He stopped and took a mouthful of coffee. Then, after a moment's hesitation, picked up a letter from one of the piles and held it out to her. 'And this.'

Scanning down the first few formal lines, Sophie frowned in confusion.

'What is it?'

'A letter from Ralph's solicitors in Hawksworth. They received this letter to forward on to me.'

He slid a folded piece of paper out from the pile and tossed it onto the desk beside her. Something in the abruptness of his movements told her that it was significant, though his face was as inscrutable as ever, his eyes opaque.

Warily Sophie picked up the thick pale blue paper and unfolded it. The script on it was even and sloping—the hand of a person who was used to writing letters rather than sending texts or emails, Sophie thought vaguely as she began to read.

My Dear Kit—
I know this letter will come as a surprise, and after all this time am not foolish enough to believe it will be a pleasant one, however I must put aside my selfish trepidation and confront things I should have dealt with a long time ago.

Sophie's heart had started to beat very hard. She glanced up at Kit, her mouth open to say something, but his head was half turned away from her as he continued working his way through the pile of post, not inviting comment. She carried on reading.

I'm sorry—that's the first thing I want to say, although those words are too little, too late. There is so much more I need to add to them. There are things I'd like to explain for my own selfish reasons, in the hope you might understand and perhaps even forgive, and other things I need to tell you that are very much in your interest. Things that will affect you now, and will go on affecting your family far into the future.

A pulse of adrenaline hit Sophie's bloodstream as she read that bit. She carried on, skimming faster now, impatient to find out what it all meant.

The last thing I want to do is pressure you for any kind of response, so on the basis that you have my address at the top of this letter and the warmest and most sincere of invitations to come here at any time to suit you, I will leave you to make your own decision.
Know, though, how much it would mean to me to see you.
Your hopeful mother
Juliet Fitzroy

Slowly Sophie put down the letter, her head spinning.

'So your mother wants you to go and see her?' she said, admittedly rather stupidly.

Kit tossed another envelope into the bin. 'So it would appear, Mr Holmes.'

'Will you go?' With shaking fingers Sophie scrabbled to

unfold the paper again, to see where exactly Juliet Fitzroy lived. 'Imlil,' she said in a puzzled voice, then read the line below on the address. 'Blimey—Morocco?'

'Exactly.' Kit sounded offhand to the point of boredom as the contents of the envelope followed it into the bin. 'It's not exactly a few stops on the District line, and I can't think what she could say that would make the trip worthwhile.'

Sophie tapped a finger against her closed lips, her thoughts racing ahead. Morocco. Heat and sand and...harem pants. Probably. In truth she didn't know an awful lot about Morocco beyond the fact that she'd always liked the sound of it and that, right now, it seemed like a very favourable alternative to Chelsea, and the oppressive atmosphere that seemed to be stifling them both in the quiet, immaculate house.

'I've always wanted to go to Morocco,' she said, with a hint of wistfulness. 'I wonder how she ended up living there? And why she's chosen to get in touch now, after all this time?'

'I assume because she knows her little secret will have been uncovered by Ralph's death.' Kit was writing something on the bottom of a letter from the bank. 'Perhaps she wants to introduce me to my real father—although that's assuming she knows who he is. There could be thousands of possible candidates for all I know.'

Oh, God. Sophie suddenly felt dizzy as she remembered a letter she had found tucked into a book in the library at Alnburgh. She'd known at the time it was wrong to read it, but one look at the first line and she'd been unable to resist. She wished now that she'd been stronger, so she wouldn't be in the position of knowing more about Kit's paternity than he did.

Getting up from the edge of the desk, she paced to the bookcase on the other side of the room, deliberately turning her back on him. 'There aren't.' She took a deep breath and closed her eyes, wincing. 'She knows.'

There was a pause. On the bookcase in front of her, between the volumes of military history and thick books on Middle Eastern politics, was a photograph. It showed a Kit she didn't know, standing in the centre of a group of men in camouflage jackets in front of an army truck.

'How do you know?'

He spoke with sinister softness. Light-headed with apprehension, Sophie turned round. 'Do you remember that day at Alnburgh, when I was…ill…?' She'd got her period and had been completely unprepared, and Kit had stepped in and taken control. She smiled faintly. 'You showed me into the library while you went to the village shop.'

'I remember.' His voice held an edge of steel that made the smile wither. 'And?'

'And I looked at the books while I was waiting.' She went over to lean against the desk beside him again, longing to touch him but not quite knowing how to. 'I found some old Georgette Heyer—she's my absolute favourite, so I took one down and opened it, and a letter fell out.' She looked down at her hands, picking at one of the ragged nails she'd meant to file before he came home. 'A love letter. It was addressed to "My Darling Juliet".'

Kit wasn't looking at her. He was staring straight ahead, out of the window, the slats of the blind casting bars of shadows on his damaged face so that he looked as if he were in a cage. When he said nothing, Sophie went on in a voice that was husky and hesitant.

'A-at first I assumed it was from Ralph and I was amazed. It was so beautifully romantic—so tender and passionate, and I just couldn't imagine him writing anything like that.'

'So who was it from?'

'I don't know. I didn't have a chance to finish it before you came back, and…' she couldn't stop herself from reaching out then, touching his cheek with the backs of her fingers as she recalled the tension that had vibrated between them '…then it kind of went out of my head for a while. I did look later, when I put the book back, but it wasn't signed with a name.'

He got to his feet, taking a few steps away from her.

'So how do you know it wasn't Ralph?'

'Because it talked about *you*,' Sophie said, very softly, standing up too. 'You must only have been tiny and he'd obviously just come back from visiting. He said how painful it was for him to leave you, knowing it was Ralph you thought of as your father.'

'Why didn't you tell me this before?' Kit demanded icily.

Sophie swallowed. 'It was none of my business at the time. I knew straight away that I shouldn't have read it, and, let's face it, we didn't exactly know each other well enough for me to drop that kind of information casually into the conversation. And then afterwards…there just wasn't the chance.' She paused, nervously moistening her lips as she gathered the courage to voice the misgivings that had been silently closing in on her since she'd woken that morning. 'I don't know, Kit, sometimes I think we hardly know each other any better now.'

Her stomach was in knots as she waited for him to reply. Standing with his back to her, his shoulders looking as if they'd been carved from granite. And then he sighed, and some of the tension went out of them.

'I'm sorry.' He turned round. 'I don't understand it, that's all. Why the hell didn't she just leave Ralph and go to be with him—whoever he was—and take me with her?'

The bitterness in his tone made her heart ache with compassion, but at the same time a part of it sang. Because anger was emotion, and because he was *talking* to her about it.

She shrugged, taking care to sound casual. 'Maybe that's what she wants to explain.' Going over to him, she stretched up to lightly kiss his lips. 'Let's go. Let's go to Morocco and find out.'

CHAPTER THREE

AND so, with her characteristic clear-sightedness, Sophie made the decision that they should go to see Juliet. All that was left for Kit to do was make the arrangements.

If it hadn't been for her he would simply have put the letter into the waste-paper bin, along with all the rest of the junk mail. He had long ago closed his heart to the woman who had walked out on him when he was six years old, promising to return. That broken promise, perhaps more than her abandonment, had sown seeds of wariness and mistrust in him that grew over the years into a forest of thorns around his heart. Sophie alone had slipped through its branches.

And in the same way, when he'd shown her the letter she had cut through the anger and bitterness and made it all seem so simple. So obvious. About facts, not emotions.

Odd that he of all people should need reminding of that.

'First class?' Sophie murmured, looking up at him from under her lashes as he steered her in the direction of the passenger lounge at London City Airport. 'How sweet of you to remember I never travel any other way.'

Her eyes sparkled, and he knew she was thinking of the way they'd met, when she'd sat opposite him—without a ticket—in the first-class carriage on the train from London to Northumberland. He'd spent the entire four-hour journey trying not to look at her, and trying to stop thinking about touching her.

It was going to be the same story today, he thought dryly. They'd spent the morning in bed, but in spite of the fact she'd managed to pack and get ready in under an hour she looked utterly delectable in loose, wide-legged white linen trousers and a grey T-shirt that showed off the outline of her gorgeous breasts.

'Not this time, I'm afraid,' he said gravely as Air Hostess Barbie came towards them, her dazzling smile faltering a little as she saw the state of his face. 'Major Fitzroy? Your plane is waiting, if you'd like to follow me.'

As she stepped onto the tarmac Sophie's eyes widened and her mouth opened as she saw the small Citation jet.

'Holy cow...' she squeaked. He couldn't stop himself from bending his head and kissing her smiling mouth.

'Major Fitzroy.' Neither of them noticed the pilot approaching until he was almost beside them. Unhurriedly Kit raised his head, but kept a hand on the small of Sophie's back as he reached out and shook the one the pilot offered.

'Good to see you, Kit.' Beneath his dark glasses the man's face broke into a grin. 'I'd like to say you're looking well, but—'

Kit nodded, automatically raising a hand to touch the cuts on his face. 'Your natural charm is outweighed by your honesty, McAllister,' he said dryly.

The pilot's expression suddenly became more serious. 'You just back from a tour?'

'Two days ago.'

Kit's tone was deliberately bland. By contrast the pilot spoke with feeling.

'I don't envy you. It's absolute hell being out there, and then almost worse coming home.'

Smoothly Kit changed the subject by turning to Sophie.

'Nick, let me introduce you to Sophie Greenham. Sophie, Nick McAllister. He's an old friend.'

'He's flattering me.' Grinning again, Nick McAllister shook Sophie's hand firmly. 'I was far too low down the pecking order to be a friend of Major Fitzroy. We served alongside each other in some fairly joyless places, until I couldn't take any more and quit to get married and do a nice, safe job.'

'Do you miss it?' Sophie asked. It was impossible not to like him, and it was always a good idea to be nice to the person who was about to fly you across Europe.

'Not in the slightest, but then I'm not made of the same heroic stuff as Kit. Leaving it all behind was the best thing I ever did, especially as my wife only agreed to marry me if I gave up. She's expecting our second child in a few days.'

Sophie felt as if something sharp had just pierced her side. 'Congratulations,' she managed in an oddly high-pitched voice.

Luckily Kit was already beginning to move away. 'In that case we'd better get going or you'll be on the way to Marrakech while she's on her way to the delivery room,' he said.

The cabin of the small plane was the most insanely luxurious thing Sophie had ever seen. Everything was in toning shades of pale caramel and crème, even the stewardess who appeared as soon as they were airborne with champagne and strawberries. It reminded Sophie of the villain's lair in a James Bond film.

'Kit Fitzroy, you big show-off,' she said, struggling to suppress a huge smile as the stewardess disappeared through the suede curtains again. 'You don't impress me with your fancy private plane, you know. Just think of your carbon footprint—how do you live with the guilt?'

'Years of practice.' He took a mouthful of champagne, and for a split second a shadow passed across his face. 'But I'd heard the recession has had an impact on business and I was selflessly prepared to put Nick's income before my carbon footprint.'

'Spoken like a true hero.' Sophie settled back in a huge cream leather seat and looked around. 'He seems happy enough that he made the right decision though,' she added casually, idly twirling a strawberry around by its stem. 'Would you ever consider…?'

'Giving up my career to get married?' Kit drawled in mock outrage. 'In *this* day and age?'

Taking a mouthful of champagne, Sophie almost snorted it out of her nose. 'Shut up,' she spluttered, laughing. 'You know what I mean.'

Suddenly his face was serious again, his silvery eyes luminous in the clear light above the clouds. 'Yes. And yes.' He gave her a twisted smile that made her stomach flip. 'I don't want to go back. The question is, do you still want to marry me?'

Below them the sea stretched in a glittering infinity. Sophie's heart soared. This was exactly the kind of conversation that had seemed so impossible in the big, empty house in Chelsea, but up here it was different. She could be herself.

'Of *course* I do,' she moaned, then added hastily, 'I mean, if that's what you want.'

He put his glass down on the gleaming wood ledge. His eyes were on hers.

'Come here,' he said softly.

She was about to mutter something about seat belts, but stopped herself just in time as she realised those kind of rules didn't apply to private planes. And anyway, she couldn't imagine anything safer than being held by Kit. She went over, settling herself sideways on his lap, her feet hanging over the arm of his seat.

'I don't need a piece of paper or anything, you know that,' she said quietly. 'I know that five months is a long time and a lot has happened since then. You've been away and…I don't know, I thought that maybe when you'd had time to think about it you might have decided it wasn't such a good idea.'

Taking a deep breath in, Kit closed his eyes and let his head fall back against the leather headrest. That was exactly what he'd decided yesterday morning, waking up beside her and realising that they were little more than strangers. Understanding that what had happened to Lewis could so easily have happened to him, and that his life wasn't the only one he was playing Russian roulette with any more.

But now, with her body folded into his, her hair soft against his jaw, the decision was abstract. Irrelevant. The rightness of his initial instinct to make her his and never let her go was indisputable.

'I haven't.' He picked up her hand, stroking his thumb over her empty third finger. 'And I need to get you a ring as soon as possible so you don't think that again.'

'A ring? Ooh—exciting! How soon can we do it?'

He couldn't stop a smile from spreading across his face as the uncertainty and darkness receded. 'Well, we can do it tomorrow if you don't mind having a ring that comes from a back alley in the souk and costs the same as a glass of Chardonnay in a pub in Chelsea, or as soon as we get home we can—'

She silenced him by kissing the corner of his mouth. 'I wouldn't mind that at all, but I didn't mean the ring. I meant how soon can we get married? Can we do it when we get home?'

He reached around her to pick up his champagne. 'I think there might be a few things you have to do first, like get a licence and book a place and a person to do it.'

She shifted her position so that she was sitting astride him. 'That can't take too long, surely?' She licked her lips and didn't quite meet his eye. 'I mean, we don't want one of those full-scale epics with a football team of bridesmaids, a cake the size of Everest and three hundred guests.'

'No? I thought that was what every bride wanted?'

He actually felt her shudder. 'Not me. Or not unless there are two hundred and ninety-nine people you want to invite, and I get to have Jasper on my side of the church.'

'You must have people you want there? Family?'

In spite of the clear light flooding the cabin her eyes had darkened to the colour of old green glass, but he only glimpsed them for a moment before her lashes swept down and hid them from view.

'I don't have family. And I certainly don't have a father to walk me down the aisle and make a touching speech recapping significant moments on my journey to being the woman in the meringue dress.'

Her tone was light enough but everything else resisted further questioning. He could feel the tension in her body, and see from the way she was avoiding his eye that they'd stumbled into a no-go area. Very gently he ran a fingertip down her cheek, tilting her face upwards when he reached her chin.

'You have a mother,' he said softly. 'And most mothers would probably say that getting to be Mother of the Bride is one of the highlights of the job.'

She slid off his knee, getting up and taking the champagne bottle from the ice bucket in which the stewardess had left it. Kit felt a moment of desolation as the contact with her body was lost.

'My mother is not most mothers,' she said in a tone of deep, self-deprecating irony as she poured champagne into her glass. Too fast—the froth surged upwards and spilled over. 'Oh, knickers—sorry,' she muttered, making a grab for it and trying to suck up the cascading fizz.

'It's fine—leave it.' Taking the glass and the bottle from her, he tilted the glass as he refilled it. 'So, why wasn't she like other mothers?'

'Well, for a start I wasn't even allowed to call her that.' She slid back into her own seat, took a mouthful of champagne before continuing, 'Not "Mother" or "Mum" or anything that would pin her into a narrow gender-stereotyped role that carried political and social associations of subservience and oppression.' She rolled her eyes elaborately and he could hear the inverted commas she put around the phrase.

'So what did you call her?'

Sophie shrugged. 'Rainbow, like everyone else.'

'Was that her name?'

'It was for as long as I can remember.' Absently she trailed her finger through the little puddle of champagne. Two lines were etched between her narrow brows, and Kit found himself longing to reach over and smooth them away. 'It was only when I went to live with my Aunt Janet when I was fifteen that I discovered her real name was Susan.'

'So why did she call herself Rainbow?'

Sighing, Sophie slumped back in the seat, her glossy maple-coloured hair bright and beautiful against the pale upholstery. Nick ought to hire her as a promo model, Kit thought wryly, then instantly dismissed the thought. Over his dead body.

'For the same reason she called me Summer, I suppose. Because it fitted in with her barmy hippy friends, and marked us out to be "alternative" and "different" and "free". Which to her, was a good thing.'

'But not to you?'

She threw him a pitying glance. 'Please. You try being the only person in the school assembly hall wearing a violently coloured stripey handknit jumper and patchwork dungarees instead of a grey skirt and a navy cardigan because your mother believes "every individual has a right to be an individual".'

She said this last bit in a tone of dreamy wistfulness that gave Kit an instant snapshot of her mother; Rainbow, the feminist, peace-campaigning free spirit. None of those were bad things to be, he reflected idly, and behind Sophie's exasperation he sensed genuine love.

'At least your mother was there,' he said wryly.

'Yes. Even if I often wished she wasn't.' She gave a swift smile that dimpled her cheeks and told him that she'd had enough of serious stuff. Through the window the sunlight had lost its dazzling golden glare and deepened to the colour of good cognac. Kit was no artist, or photographer, but looking at Sophie as she leaned her chin on her cupped hand he wished he were.

'So when are we seeing her? Juliet, I mean.'

'Tomorrow evening.' He grimaced. 'She did invite us to stay with her, but I politely declined. I've booked us into a hotel in Marrakech, and we'll drive out there for dinner.'

'How was it—talking to her?'

Kit thought. Hearing her voice had been strange, but in an abstract way. It didn't affect him any more. Sophie had healed so much of the damage she had done to him.

'It was brief and to the point, as I hope seeing her will be. This isn't about her, or rebuilding a relationship. I just want answers.'

'About your father?'

'Yes.'

Reaching to pick up his glass, Kit was aware again of the burning numbness in his fingers. It came and went, but there was no doubt he'd felt it for the first time on this last tour, since he'd found out that Ralph Fitzroy wasn't his father. Maybe finding out who he was would stop the feeling that he was dissolving.

He was saved from having to say any more by the appearance of the colour-coordinated stewardess, bearing plates of canapés.

'Captain McAllister hopes you're enjoying the flight, and

asked me to tell you that we'll be landing at Marrakech-Menara in just over an hour.'

In the seat opposite Sophie arched her back and unfolded the leg that she'd had tucked up beneath her on the seat. Her bare foot brushed his knee.

'Thanks,' Kit said blandly to the stewardess as lust lashed through him. 'Can you ask him if he can go any faster?'

CHAPTER FOUR

THEY stepped down from the plane into a rose and indigo evening. Sophie almost hadn't wanted the flight to end, but it was impossible not to feel excited when she'd looked out of the window and seen Marrakech below. 'The Red City', they called it, and in the light of the dying sun it was easy to see why.

A porter went ahead of them into the terminal building with their luggage while Nick waited on the tarmac to say goodbye. He and Kit shook hands, agreeing that Kit would be in touch to arrange a return flight, then he turned to Sophie.

'Enjoy Morocco.' He grinned.

'I will.' She already was. The air was as warm and thick as soup, and as spicily fragrant. She breathed it in and impulsively reached up and gave him a quick hug. 'Thank you for bringing us.'

In the airport building Kit went to change money and she looked around, her pulse quickening as she listened to the unfamiliar languages filling the magnificent and curiously cathedral-like space. She loved travelling, and this was the feeling she always got in a new place—a sense of promise, of discoveries waiting to be made and adventures yet to be had.

'Ready?' he asked huskily.

Their eyes met and she nodded, torn between the desire to

rush to the nearest hotel with him, and the urge to get out and explore the city that lay tantalisingly just beyond the soaring criss-crossed pillars of the terminal building.

Kit walked ahead of her, stuffing the wad of dirhams he had just exchanged into the back pocket of his jeans. Sophie's throat dried with instant lust, and along with it the glib warning she was about to give him about the danger of pickpockets. No one would mess with Kit.

A car from their hotel was waiting for them, sleek and gleaming amongst the battered, dusty taxis. The driver got out, nodding respectfully at Kit as he came round to open the door for them. Smiling shyly, Sophie slid into the car while Kit spoke to the driver in rapid, fluent French and tipped the porter who had brought out their bags.

Another gush of desire crashed through Sophie, and she leaned back against the seat, inwardly outraged at her own weakness as Kit got in beside her. She was the girl who'd always prided herself on her independence, her ability to go anywhere and do anything on her own, and here she was being treated like some fragile princessy type, cosseted from the need to take control of anything.

God, it was sexy though. As the car moved through wide streets that, despite the lateness of the hour, were still choked with vehicles, freed from the need to be responsible she felt deliciously reckless. Maybe it was too much free champagne on the aeroplane. Or maybe it was just Kit—the intoxicating effect of his strength and assurance. His *masculinity*. Not to mention his knee-weakening gorgeousness and the memory of what he'd done to her earlier with the chocolate spread…

'Djamaa El Fna.' Kit's husky voice close to her ear half roused her out of her thoughts, half plunged her deeper into them. 'Marrakech's famous square.'

Suppressing a shiver of longing, she turned to look out of the window. The dusk was lit up with the strings of lights swinging beneath the canopies of stalls, and the flames from braziers. Wreaths of smoke blurred the lights into orbs of brightness, which highlighted the faces of the stallholders and gave the scene an atmosphere of theatre. Even from inside the car Sophie could smell roasting meat and spices and hear a rapid, frantic drumbeat. It seemed to reach down inside her, echoing the primitive, restless thud of her own heart.

She turned to Kit. His face was shadowed, but the lights from the square made his eyes gleam like beaten silver.

'Let's get out,' she said breathlessly. 'I want to see it.'

Kit said something to the driver and the car pulled to the side of the road. Sophie had reached for the door handle and was opening the door before the car had even stopped.

It was like nothing she'd ever seen or experienced before. The rhythm of the drums shimmered down her spine, making her hips move instinctively as she moved forwards. She could feel herself smiling as the heat of the night melted bones that felt as if they'd been frozen for a long, long time. From behind Kit hooked an arm around her neck, drawing her back against the hard wall of his body.

'Slow down, gypsy girl,' he murmured into her hair. 'I don't want to lose you.'

She twisted herself around so that she was facing him. The lights shone in eyes that were dark with excitement. They looked like pools of reflected stars.

'I'm not going anywhere without you.' She smiled, moving her hands down to his hips and sliding her fingers into the pockets of his jeans, pulling him against her. He could feel her hips moving, snake-like, as if the music weren't just all around them, but was inside her too.

Dangerous thought.

'If you carry on doing that, the only place you'll be going is back to the hotel, as quickly as possible,' he growled, pulling away, capturing her hands and drawing her with him as he began to walk forwards.

She was like a chameleon, he thought. Wherever you put

her she had a way of adapting, becoming part of the scene. For a second he thought of what the other women he'd dated, with their expensive shoes and glossy Knightsbridge hair, would make of this place. The idea brought a smile to his lips.

'Come on, I'm hungry,' she said, pulling on his hand. Her excitement was completely infectious. The smile widened.

'What do you want to eat?'

He had to bend down and speak close to her ear to make himself heard above the noise of the marketplace. The scent of her made his head spin and took him back to earlier, on the kitchen worktop. London seemed like another lifetime, but in that moment the two worlds collided and desire rushed through him, dilating his veins with heat.

'Do you think anywhere sells chocolate spread?' she asked innocently.

'Stop it,' he warned.

She laughed, turning and beginning to walk between the crowded stalls again. Her hair hung loose down her back, gleaming in the lights as she turned to look at the displays of jewel-coloured fruit and golden, deep-fried prawns and tiny pastries. Kit didn't really take in the food on offer. He was too busy looking at her high, rounded bottom beneath the thin linen trousers, which was far lusher than any of the pomegranates and melons on display.

The music got louder as they approached a break in the stalls where a group of musicians had gathered, squatting on the ground around their framedrums and reed-like pipes, a woman in silken robes undulating in front of them. Sophie's pace slowed, and fragrant smoke wreathed her as she turned to face him. The bright lights beneath the canopies made her skin glow gold and her eyes, as she looked up at him, were dark and dilated.

'I don't know where to start. There's so much I want to try.'

Food, Kit reminded himself sternly. She's talking about

food. Reaching out, he brushed his thumb over her slightly parted lips.

'What do you feel like?'

Looking up into his eyes, she shrugged slowly. 'Anything that I haven't tried before. Something that'll blow my mind.'

Kit dragged his gaze away from her. The smoke was coming from a stall opposite that was laid out with just about every kind of local delicacy, both tempting and alarming, and a man standing behind it, impassively laying skeins of small sausages onto a searing hot grill. Kit spoke to him, and he glanced at Sophie, his dark eyes gleaming with approval as he took the money Kit offered.

'What did you ask for?'

'You'll just have to wait and see,' he said gruffly. 'Close your eyes.'

Hesitantly, Sophie did as she was told. The noise around her seemed to increase as darkness flooded her head, and the scent of cedar smoke and spices and meat and garlic and hot, salty bread intensified so that her mouth was instantly alive. And beneath it all, close and strong and most delicious of all, was the scent of Kit's skin as he raised his hand to her lips.

'Are you ready?'

She nodded. A great happiness was simmering inside her, threatening to bubble over. She was in love with the moment, the place, the man she was with and everything seemed sharply, almost painfully wonderful. Tentatively she opened her mouth, her senses on high alert, both afraid and excited.

She breathed in chilli-scented steam for a second, then tasted something strong, spicy, smoky-rich on her tongue and guessed it was one of the tiny local sausages she'd seen the man put on the grill.

'Mmm…gorgeous,' she murmured, swallowing and opening her eyes. 'More, please.'

Kit towered above her; inscrutable, beautiful. The cuts and bruising on his face seemed less noticeable here somehow;

perhaps because everything was more real, more raw than in England. The painted sign that swung above the stall was chipped and rusting, the face of the woman at the next stall was creased like crumpled paper, her smile gap-toothed, joyful.

'Close your eyes. Keep them closed.'

Sophie pressed her lips together holding back her own smile. Kit's fingertips on her lips made a shiver of longing travel down her spine.

'Open your mouth.'

He dropped a fat olive onto her tongue and she held it between her teeth for a second, enjoying the feel of its skin on her tongue-tip before biting into it with an explosion of flavour. A dense, dry lamb kefteh followed, then a slice of tomato, slippery with olive oil and mint leaves. Gripping the metal pole of the canopy, she kept her eyes closed as he'd said, giving herself up to the succession of sensations and flavours, murmuring her appreciation as oil moistened her lips and dripped down her chin. The music and the drums and the warm, smoky air wrapped around them, so that it was easy to imagine it was just her and Kit, alone under the dark blue African sky...

Easy, but perhaps not wise. There was a throbbing at the apex of her thighs and her skin was so sensitive that the lightest touch of his fingers brought goosebumps up on her bare arms.

'Enough?'

Kit's voice was a husky whisper, but she could hear the amusement in it. Her senses sang. She shook her head.

'More.'

More quickly now he fed her bread, soft and airily dissolving beneath its hard crust, meltingly tender meat, battered prawns and crisp fried squid. She pulled a face as she chewed that, and next he gave her something spicy loaded onto bread that made her lips tingle.

'Mmm…better…' she murmured.

'What about this? Open wide…'

Juice, redolent of cumin and garlic, ran onto her tongue and a second later she felt something lightly touch her lips. With a low moan of greed she opened them, trying to capture it as it quivered just out of reach. She heard Kit laugh, a low throaty sound that made her longing crank up another notch. Sticking her tongue out, she caught whatever it was he was holding, his fingers with it, sucking them hard until he let it go.

It was like nothing she'd tasted before—soft, but at the same time oddly tough and with an earthy flavour that she couldn't name. She swallowed.

'What was it?'

He brought his head down so his lips grazed the lobe of her ear, and let them linger.

'Snail.'

Her eyes flew open. 'Really?'

'Well, when you didn't object to the sheep's head…'

'Kit! You—'

Laughing, he caught her wrist as she went to hit him, and it was then that she noticed the crowd of people—locals in djellabas, curious tourists, the musicians from opposite—standing around her in a circle, watching. They burst into a round of applause, and the man came round from behind the stall to shake her hand, clearly delighted to have such excellent free advertising.

Sophie looked up at Kit, smiling sweetly, speaking so softly only he could hear. 'You are in *such trouble* when we get to the hotel.'

Kit's teeth showed white as he flashed her a grin. 'I can't wait.'

Taking advantage of the assembled crowd, the musicians started up again. Sophie wondered when they'd stopped. The dancing girl came forward, holding her hands out. Her face was half veiled and above it her dark eyes warm and melting. Sophie took the hands she offered, casting a deliberately wicked look over her shoulder at Kit.

'You might have to…'

'Sophie—'

Already she had slipped her little jewelled ballet flats off and Kit felt his smile set like concrete as desire kicked him in the ribs. He stood back helplessly and watched her move to the centre of the circle of people, tying her shirt above her midriff then raising her arms above her head like the Berber girl, rotating her hips.

Of course, he knew she'd be good at it. But she wasn't just good. She was…hypnotic. She didn't have the technical precision of the other girl with her intricate moves, but there was a more earthy sensuality about the way she undulated. The circle of onlookers thickened, became two deep as the beat got faster, the musicians responding to the writhing bodies of the two women—one veiled and mysterious, the other fiery and sensual. Kit couldn't take his eyes off Sophie's midriff, the snake-like undulations of her flesh.

Where had she learned how to do that? And why hadn't she shown him before now? In the privacy of a bedroom where it wouldn't take every shred of his self-control to subdue his raging erection and withstand the urge to hoist her over his shoulder in a fireman's lift and bear her away.

Night had descended properly now and a full moon floated high up in the sky like a white balloon. The crowd was pressing in closer. In the glow of the lamps the musicians wore rapt, trance-like expressions on their faces. Sophie was half turned away from him now. Her face was hidden by her hair, but he could see the rise and fall of her chest as she breathed hard, see the gleam of moisture on her skin.

Kit couldn't wait any longer. She had had her revenge. Going forwards, he slid his arm around her waist and pulled her into his body, scooping her up in one swift, decisive movement.

She didn't resist. Tipping her head back, she looked at him with eyes that glittered like black diamonds.

'Time to find the hotel, I think,' he said grimly, turning and heading away from the little clapping, whooping crowd.

The music got fainter, swallowed up by the sounds of the market. Stretching up, Sophie pressed her lips to the column of his throat, where a pulse was beating with the same insistence as the fading drum.

'I thought you'd never ask.'

The car was cool and quiet after the sultry, throbbing air outside. They carefully didn't touch, sitting at opposite ends of the wide seat, knowing that any physical contact would be dangerous—like putting a lighted match into a box of fireworks.

Looking at each other was bad enough. But Sophie couldn't take her eyes off him. The ten minutes it took to get to the hotel seemed like a lot longer.

The car slid to a halt in front of an unassuming building—little more than a huge, arched wooden door, flanked by lemon trees, set into a wall. The driver got out and walked round to open the passenger doors.

'Leave this to me,' Kit growled.

Sophie was about to ask what he was talking about, but he'd already got out of the car and come quickly round to her side. Leaning in and sliding one arm around her shoulders, the other beneath her knees, he pulled her against his chest again.

'Kit, I can—'

'Shh.'

His face was set and there was a muscle flickering in his jaw. Sophie let herself go pliant in his arms, but had to clamp her teeth together to stop herself from moaning out loud as he carried her towards an imposing and ancient-looking set of wooden doors. She could feel his erection pressing against her hip.

'Are you by any chance using me as a human shield?' she murmured.

His lips twitched into a momentary smile, but then it was gone and his face resumed its deadpan expression as the driver who had brought them opened one of the giant-sized wooden doors.

Sophie had to admire Kit's cool. Aside from keeping her rampaging desire in check she also had to try to stop her jaw from dropping at the sheer magnificence of her surroundings. The door had opened into a courtyard, surrounded on all sides by cloisters of pure white stone that, in the blue dimness, looked like sugar-icing. A rectangular pool stretched the length of the courtyard, and beyond it light spilled through another arched doorway, spreading golden ripples onto the water. Candles in glass lanterns were placed at intervals along it, their flames dipping as Kit passed, as if they were bowing.

The contrast with the vibrant chaos of the night market couldn't have been greater.

A woman of quite extraordinary beauty appeared in the doorway.

'Welcome to Dar Roumana.'

Her long black hair was fastened back from her olive-skinned, heart-shaped face and she was dressed in some kind of simple white linen shift. Gosh, thought Sophie weakly. The whole thing really had taken on the aspect of an Arabian Nights–type fantasy. She wouldn't have been surprised if a genie had swept down on a flying carpet.

'It's Kit Fitzroy. I have a reservation, but my wife is feeling faint. If you could show us to our room I'll check in properly later.'

'Of course.'

Sophie bit her lip to stop herself smirking. Faint with lust, possibly. They followed her into the lamplit room, where she took down a large silver key from a row of hooks on the wall behind a desk, then up a curving staircase and into a high stone corridor that overlooked the courtyard below. Tiny candles in glass votives were placed along the tiled floor, throwing their flickering shadows onto the walls as they went.

How could shadows look so erotic?

'Here is your room.'

Turning the key, the dark-haired woman opened the door and stood back respectfully. 'My name is Malika. If there is anything I can do for you…'

'That's very kind,' Kit said curtly, 'but there's nothing for now.'

'Some mint tea, for your wife, if she is ill…?'

'Oh…th-thanks, but I'll be fine,' Sophie squeaked. 'I just need to lie down.'

Malika retreated, closing the door silently.

The second she'd gone Kit gave a low, animal-sounding moan and Sophie wriggled free from his arms, sliding to the floor as their mouths met and their bodies collided, limbs tangling as they struggled to free each other of their clothes.

'Just need…to…lie down,' Sophie gasped when their open mouths parted long enough for Kit to pull her top over her head. Wildly she looked around, too dazed with the immediacy of her need to be naked and horizontal to take in the spectacular suite.

'Through here,' Kit growled, heading towards a set of double doors inlaid with silver, through which it was just possible to see a low bed, made up in white linen and piled high with cushions. However, they'd only got halfway when she took off her bra and he had to pull her into his arms and kiss her again, splaying his hands over her warm bare back before dipping his head and tracing the tip of his tongue around one rosy nipple.

The sound she made was almost one of pain. He felt her

body stiffen and arch beneath his hands and took her into his mouth as her fingers slid into his hair, twisting, pulling.

It had only been a matter of hours since they'd made love in bed at home, but his need to have her again was as sharp and all-consuming as if he'd been starved of sex for a year. Being in such close proximity to her on the plane, putting food in her mouth in the marketplace and seeing the sensual absorption with which she'd tasted it had cranked his desire up to an uncomfortable level. Watching her dance had tipped him over the edge of uncomfortable and into full-on pain.

A series of shudders rocked her and she cried out, wrenching herself away and hauling him up so she could reach the fastening of his trousers. Her hands were shaking and when one accidentally brushed against his erection he almost came.

'I have a feeling…' she breathed raggedly, taking hold of his pulsing length '…that this is going to be *quick*.'

'What gave you that idea?' he rasped through gritted teeth, yanking her trousers open so that buttons bounced over the tiled floor.

'Not sure…'

There was the sound of ripping fabric as she struggled to free herself of the thin linen trousers. A second later there was another as he didn't bother to struggle to free her of her knickers.

Both naked, they gazed at each other for a second, their breathing loud and rapid. And then he was taking hold of her shoulders, fastening his mouth to hers, hitching her up against him as he carried her to the low bed.

They fell on it together. With the same kind of sensual flick of her hips he had seen her do when she was dancing she moved so she was astride him.

The room had a single huge window, covered with a kind of wooden fretwork shutter that cast intricate shadows over her naked body. Eyes half closed, she gazed down at him, her face haughty and abstracted as she raised herself up onto her knees and took him inside her. Kit bit back a cry, clenching his teeth with the effort of not letting go.

'Don't fight it,' she breathed, moving her hips. 'Don't hold back—I want you—'

He took her waist in his hands, holding her as she rode him, not taking his eyes off her face. Then he let one hand slip down to the place where their bodies joined.

He only had to brush her clitoris with his thumb to precipitate the orgasm that had been building with each hard, neat flick of her hips. And as her mouth opened and her eyes closed in ecstasy he felt a moment of pure, clear joy and finally gave in to his own wild climax.

She sank down on top of him, their skin sticky with sweat, their hearts thudding against each other. And for the first time in a long time Kit slipped easily into sleep, completely at peace.

CHAPTER FIVE

THE call to prayer echoed out from minarets across the city; a thin wail, crescendoing to a discordant chorus that floated through the limpid dawn.

Kit's eyes flew open, his body catapulting into a sitting position.

For a moment he didn't move. His heart was pounding, his skin covered with an icy sweat. The bedroom was bathed in the melting Turkish-delight pink of a perfect dawn, and beside him Sophie slept on. Half draped in a white linen sheet, she looked like a voluptuous goddess from some rococo-painted ceiling, and for a moment his panic ebbed as he watched the gentle rise and fall of her chest as she breathed.

Marrakech, he reminded himself. He was in *Marrakech*. Off duty.

He exhaled heavily, easing himself back onto the pillows. The pins-and-needles sensation in his hands was back again. The call to prayer continued, a plaintive refrain that took Kit back and made him remember all the things that last night had made him so comprehensively forget.

God.

His heart lurched and instantly he was out of bed, looking round for his phone. He had *wanted* to forget the heat and the sweat and the constant, low-key adrenaline. He had wanted to forget walking along that road to the bridge where the bomb was half concealed in a tangle of scrubby weeds and rubbish. But Lewis…

What right did he have to forget about him?

'Kit?' From the bed Sophie's voice was as warm and thick as honey. He tensed against it.

'It's OK. Go back to sleep.' He found his phone from the pocket of his kicked-aside jeans and headed for the door to the terrace. 'I need to make a phone call, then I'll order breakfast.'

Sophie turned over onto her stomach, burying her face into pillows that were still warm and breathing in the scent of him. Him and sex. It was a delicious and intoxicating combination. Happiness seeped through her, a gentler echo of the wild bliss she'd felt last night, and the day stretched out ahead, ripe with promised pleasure. Beyond the walls of the hotel she could almost sense the city that had already so enthralled her waking up, drawing her out.

It would have to wait, she thought drowsily. Breakfast first, and then she had plans for Kit in the Olympic-swimming-pool-sized marble bath…

She drew her knees up to her chest, hugging her stomach. Last night had been the most rapturous sex of her life and she couldn't help wondering whether the joy she'd felt was simply from the earth-shattering orgasm Kit had given her, or something even more magical…

Talking to him about her childhood on the plane yesterday, she had finally understood just how much she had wanted the normal, settled family life that other people took for granted. She couldn't turn the clock back, but she felt now as if she'd been given another chance. A new start, to create a secure family unit of her own. With Kit, in a beautiful sunny house somewhere, that they would fill with treasures from their travels, and children. Lots of children…

At that moment anything seemed possible, and as she drifted back into sleep she was smiling.

* * *

The sun was high overhead in a sky as hard and polished and blue as the little inlaid tiles that decorated the walls of the buildings and little cafés that lined the dusty streets.

The densely packed stalls of last night had been cleared away from the city's main square, but the wide expanse was still filled with performers, medicine men, acrobats and orange juice sellers. Kit was aware of Sophie taking everything in with wide-eyed delight. She was wearing a narrow, ankle-skimming dress in white muslin, and with her hair tied in a loose knot at the back of her head and brass bangles jangling on her wrist she looked completely at home.

'It reminds me of the music festivals I used to go to with Rainbow when I was a child,' she said, lacing her fingers through his. 'Oh, look—there's even a tarot reader! Rainbow would have been all over that.'

Kit said nothing. It reminded him of the place he'd just left. The place where Lewis's blood had glistened blackly as it soaked into the sand. There had been no change, the nurse had told him over the phone earlier. They were keeping Lewis sedated to give his body the best chance of healing, so it was impossible to tell what the long-term damage was yet. They'd have a better idea tomorrow.

Kit pushed sweat-damp hair back from his forehead with a hand that was completely numb, but steady. It was only inside that he was shaking.

He had woken from one nightmare and walked straight into another, and there was no escaping this one. It was the heat, the punishing sun, the dark eyes looking at him from beneath headscarves and veils. It was the man hauling a fresh sheep's carcass on his shoulder, the scent of blood filling the narrow alley as he passed. It was the groups of men standing in doorways, watching.

Watching. For a moment he thought he could hear that voice in his earpiece again.

Sophie slowed in front of a snake charmer playing a whiny-sounding instrument to a resolutely impassive cobra. Seeing her looking at him, the snake charmer nudged the basket with his foot. With visible reluctance the snake roused itself, desultorily swaying for a few bars before subsiding again. Sophie gave a shout of laughter.

'Oh, poor snake! She's about as enthusiastic as a bored nightclub hostess performing for a crowd of ageing businessmen.'

Kit smiled, pressing the palm of his hand onto the middle of her back.

'You're burning.'

'I can't be. You applied the cream very thoroughly…' She looked up at him with eyes that glittered with mischief.

'Twice, in fact.' The first time it had got rubbed off all over the sheets when, hopelessly aroused, they'd fallen back onto the bed.

'And how is it fair that I'm burning in factor fifty when you don't even have cream on?' she asked huskily.

He wound a tendril of flame-coloured hair that had escaped from the knot around his finger.

'You're more sensitive than I am. Come on.' He pulled her forwards, away from the snake charmer with his steady black stare. 'Let's get out of the sun. Preferably by going back to the hotel.'

Sophie laughed, quickening her pace to keep up with him. 'No way,' she said firmly. 'I want to see more. I love it here.'

She steered him into one of the souk's dim alleyways, out of the blowtorch heat of the sun. Adrenaline stung through Kit's veins as his gaze automatically scanned the street.

'Oh, look—'

Sophie's voice reached him as if from a long distance. He turned his head automatically to see what she was pointing out to him, but was aware only of shadowed doorways where a sniper could hide, flat roofs that would provide the perfect position for a gunman to take aim.

'These are beautiful…'

She had gone over to a stall that was hung with silk clothing and was running her fingers down an olive-green scarf threaded with gold, lifting one corner so that a shaft of sunlight shone through the gossamer fabric. Kit gritted his teeth and rubbed a hand over his eyes, forcing back the blackness.

What the hell was wrong with him? It was pathetic. He had to get a grip.

'Put it on.'

His voice was hoarse, his fingers fizzing as he took down the scarf and laid it over her hair. Winding it gently around her neck in the Eastern way, he focused on the shape of her lips and the scent of her skin to stop his mind from wandering back along those dark and twisting pathways. She was here and she was real, and with the scarf around her head she looked oddly demure and very beautiful. Desire kneed him in the groin and a wave of relief and passionate gratitude swept through him. He took her face in his hands and fastened his mouth on hers.

Kissing her anchored him. His hands, now they were holding her, felt normal again and the darkness in his head was benevolent once more, filled with images from last night, of her body, tattooed by shadows as she kneeled astride him. As always, her desire rose to meet his and he felt her move towards him so that her breasts were brushing his chest.

With a muffled curse he pulled away.

'Don't stop,' she murmured, her eyes still closed and her face tipped up to his.

'If I don't I'll be taking that dress off right here and making love to you on a pile of silk cushions,' he said gruffly, 'and they're pretty strict about that here.'

She looked down, biting her lip.

Gently he unwound the scarf and picked up a tunic in the same colour. The shopkeeper had emerged from the back of his cave-like stall and was looking at them expectantly. His

face was seamed with age, his dark stare gimlet-sharp but
friendly enough. There was no trace of the suspicion and
mistrust Kit saw in people's eyes when he was in uniform.
So why was his heart beating faster, his fingers buzzing and
nerveless?

He suddenly felt inexpressibly weary. This morning he
had been eaten up with guilt for putting it all behind him and
forgetting. Now he knew that if he didn't, the remembering
would drive him mad.

If he wasn't there already.

He handed the money over without bothering to haggle and
went back to Sophie, draping the scarf around her shoulders.

'Now, Salome,' he said dryly, 'if I tell you that the hotel has
a highly recommended hammam, can I tempt you to come
back with me?'

Lying on her tummy in the dense, smoky heat of the Dar
Roumana's hammam, Sophie closed her eyes and tried to
empty her mind, focusing on nothing but the sensation of
warm oiled hands moving across her back.

The trouble was her mind didn't want to be empty. It was
too full of Kit, and if she let her guard down the hands of
the masseuse would reawaken the rapture in which he had
drenched her. When they'd got back from the souk, hot and
dusty, he had stripped her off and carried her into the enormous walk-in rainshower. Turning the setting to 'mist', they
had lain on the limestone tiles and wordlessly drunk each
other in.

But he hadn't *talked* to her, hissed a nasty little voice in
her head. From the moment they'd woken up this morning
she'd sensed a kind of tension in him, which had become increasingly obvious in the souk earlier. When she tried to ask
what was bothering him he brushed her off, so she still had
no idea what demons crouched at his back or what had put
them there.

She was so lost in thought that it was a moment before she realised that the masseuse had stopped rubbing her back. Sophie opened her eyes. Gracefully the girl unfurled a towel and held it out to her.

'Time for wash now.'

'Wash?' Thinking of the shower, Sophie was about to say that wouldn't be necessary.

'Is Moroccan hammam speciality. This way.'

Hastily doing up the clasp of her bikini top, Sophie followed her into a hexagonal room whose pale marble walls dripped with moisture. A huge marble slab stood, altar-like, in the centre of the space. Climbing onto it, Sophie felt like an offering.

The heat was intense. Rivulets of sweat dripped down her back. The girl scooped a bowl of water out of a wooden bucket and tipped it over her shoulders. Sophie tucked her knees up and rested her chin on them, submitting to her ministrations like an obedient child.

She had thought that getting away from London would make it easier. Perhaps he just needed time, she thought wistfully, allowing the masseuse to take hold of her arm and soap it from wrist to shoulder. Sophie had spent enough time on film sets to understand the bond created when people were thrown together in an intense environment. She knew the feeling of disorientation when returning to real life in the outside world, when for a while it felt impossible to connect with anyone who wasn't there.

For Kit, returning from a war zone rather than a film set, that feeling must be intensified a thousandfold. She knew how concerned he was about the boy who was hurt. Surely he would talk to her when he was ready?

Having soaped her upper body all over, the masseuse took up an innocuous-looking sponge. Sophie stiffened and gave a little cry of surprise and pain as the girl began to rub her shoulders with it and she realised it was made of something scratchy. Sandpaper perhaps. Or steel wool.

She bit her lip. It hurt, but at the same time it felt good. Like loving Kit.

Defiantly she gritted her teeth against the pain.

He loved her too—every touch, every kiss told her that. Words were unnecessary. Didn't their bodies say it all?

Kit reached the end of the long swimming pool and surfaced for air before twisting beneath the water to begin another length.

In that brief second he got a glimpse of the faded sky and realised that he'd been in the water for a long time. Initially he had focused all his energy on not thinking—on forgetting about Lewis and what had happened in the medina that morning—and instead thought of nothing beyond blankly counting the number of lengths. After a while even that blurred into meaninglessness and he just swam.

And that was what you had to do, he told himself wearily, ploughing through the water. You just had to keep going, keep shutting it out and eventually it would go away. An image of Lewis's girlfriend hung in the greenish water in front of his eyes for a second before he pushed it away with a stroke of his arm.

He couldn't spill it all out to Sophie. She was so sweet and sure and easy-going; there was no way he was going to inflict on her the dark thoughts that kept him awake at nights and had now begun to seep into his waking hours too. He'd sort it out alone, in his own way.

Reaching the other end of the pool, he broke the surface of the water again, took a lungful of air and was just about to turn around again when a movement caught his eye.

Sophie was coming down the path from the hotel, the afternoon sun making her hair dance with auburn lights and turning her skin to warm honey. She was wearing the embroidered tunic they'd bought earlier, a thick leather belt slung around her hips, and as she walked the thin silk rippled against her, showing off every line and curve. Suddenly his body seemed to forget that it was sated from the most intense sex of his life and that he'd been swimming for heaven knew how long.

If only his head were as good at overlooking stuff.

As she got nearer she raised a hand to shield her eyes from the sun, and the hem of the tunic rose to reveal another inch of pale gold thigh.

'Aren't you forgetting something?'

'I've been trying to forget a lot of things,' he drawled, vaulting out of the pool and looking her over speculatively as he reached for a towel. 'It's a whole lot easier now you've appeared looking like that.'

'Like what?' she asked distractedly, looking down at the olive-green silk tunic and frowning. 'Oh—yes, I know, this is far too short to wear on its own, but I'm going to wait until the last minute to put on my white trousers or—'

He reached out a dripping hand and took hold of her chin, tipping her face up and stopping her from saying any more.

'Like you've been lit up from the inside.'

It was true. Maybe it was the low, syrupy sunlight or some clever kind of cosmetic he knew nothing about, or maybe it was just her smile and the sparkle of her eyes and the sheen on her hair, but she seemed to glow. To radiate beauty.

She rolled her eyes. 'Ah. That would be the industrial sander the masseuse used to remove the top five layers of my skin.'

Kit slid his hand up her arm, beneath the loose sleeve. 'So underneath this you're even more naked than before?' he asked, lazily caressing her skin as he smiled into her eyes.

'You could say that… But we don't have time. That's what I came to remind you—that it's nearly six o'clock. We need to go.'

Of course. To meet the mother he hadn't seen for almost

thirty years. That was the other thing he'd been trying to forget.

You could only go on blocking things out for so long. It all caught up with you in the end.

CHAPTER SIX

THE Atlas mountains gleamed like icebergs in the distance, their snowy caps stained pink in the setting sun. Leaning back against the front seat of the huge Mercedes Kit had borrowed from the hotel, Sophie felt its last rays warm her face and kept her eyes fixed straight ahead.

Apart from the mountains, there wasn't much to see—just an endless stretch of dry red earth sparsely covered with even dryer khaki-coloured scrub—but she had to focus on something so that she didn't keep turning to look at Kit. His big hands, powerful on the steering wheel. His deep golden-brown forearms against the white linen shirt he wore with the sleeves rolled back. The way his thigh muscles rippled when he changed gear. His profile—stern, distant, perfect.

'You're staring at me,' he remarked with a faint smile, not taking his eyes from the road.

'Sorry.' Hastily Sophie looked away. 'I was trying not to.'

Kit ran a hand over his face, rubbing his fingertips tentatively over the worst of the gashes on his cheekbones. 'Let's hope she's not expecting some clean-cut merchant banker in chinos and an Oxford shirt,' he drawled with heavy irony, 'because if so she's going to be *very* disappointed.'

'You could never disappoint anyone. I, on the other hand...'

Flipping down the sun-visor, Sophie peered despondently at her own face in the little mirror. Why had she thought it was a good idea to be flayed with a pan scourer? Her skin wasn't so much lit up from the inside as on fire. She grabbed her make-up bag and took out a bottle of foundation to tone down her scarlet cheeks, but as she went to squirt some into her hand the car bounced over a pothole and a jet of ivory-rose skin-firming make-up, complete with SPF and AHAs and probably a PhD or two, gushed out onto her trousers.

Her *white* trousers.

She let out a wail of dismay, and began scrubbing at it with the ragged remains of a tissue, instantly making it about five times worse. 'What am I going to do now?'

Kit glanced across. 'Take them off. I told you you didn't need them anyway—it looks even better without.'

'To you, maybe, but that's because your judgment is clouded by testosterone. I don't think that wearing a knicker-skimming minidress is something most etiquette experts would advise when meeting one's prospective mother-in-law for the first time. She'll think I'm, I don't know…some kind of…tart.'

Running out of steam, she stopped scrubbing and looked at Kit. He was staring ahead, his face perfectly blank, but there was a muscle twitching in his jaw and on the steering wheel his knuckles showed white through the bronzed skin of his hands.

'This is the woman who cheated on her husband and let him bring up another man's child while she ran off with her lover, remember? I hardly think she's in a position to *judge* anyone.'

Sophie's heart skipped a beat at the ice that edged his words. She sensed a tiny crack had opened up in the dam that held back his emotion. She hesitated, moistening her lips, afraid of saying the wrong thing, of driving him into himself again.

'How well do you remember her?' She kept her voice as casual as possible, dabbing at the stain on her trousers again in the hope that it would look as if she were just making idle conversation.

'I don't remember much about her at all,' he said tersely. 'I was only six when she left.' There was a pause. Sophie put her head down, though she wanted so much to look at him, to touch him, but she knew there was a far greater chance of making him clam up again if she did.

'I remember her perfume,' he said with rusty reluctance. 'And I remember that I thought she was very beautiful. I also remember her saying goodbye.'

Sophie couldn't stop herself from lifting her head to look at him then.

'Oh, Kit—that must have been terrible.'

His face was still inscrutable, his heavy-lidded eyes narrowed as he kept them fixed on the empty slash of black tarmac in front of them.

'Not at the time. She promised she'd be back soon. She'd been away before...' his mouth twisted into a kind of smile '...living at Alnburgh you'd have to or else you'd go mad—so I had no reason not to believe her. She told me to look after the castle while she was away, because it was going to be mine one day. I'm not sure now if that was wishful thinking or deliberate deceit.'

Sophie turned to look out of the window. The empty scrubland had given way to softer terrain now—grassland where cows stood in languorous groups and horses grazed, their shadows long and spindly-legged in the sinking sun. Up ahead clusters of houses clung to the hillside: tiers of reddish brown interspersed by tall palm trees.

'She was probably trying to—I don't know, soften the blow a bit.'

Kit gave a hollow laugh. 'Believe me, if there's going to be a blow it's better to feel the pain and deal with it.'

He dragged a hand through his hair, making it stand up at the front, and showing the lighter streaks where the sun had bleached it. Sophie's stomach constricted with lust and she looked away quickly.

'Is that where she lives, up there?' she asked, gesturing to the village on the hill.

'Yes.'

He might be utterly unmoved, but she was suddenly nervous enough for both of them. The stain on her jeans seemed to have spread in diameter and intensified in colour. Impulsively, she kicked off her little gold sandals and frantically tried to wriggle out of her trousers without undoing the seat belt.

'What are you doing?'

'Taking these off. I think tarty is better than dirty, although—'

Assailed by doubt, she broke off and bit her lip. Kit sighed.

'Why are you so bothered by what she thinks? And so determined to make excuses for her?'

Sophie took a deep breath in, pressing down on her midriff to quell the cloud of butterflies that had risen there.

'I just want her to like me,' she said quietly. *To approve*, corrected a mocking voice inside her head. *To not see you as the grubby girl from the hippy camp.* She tugged down the green silk tunic and lifted her chin an inch. 'And I suppose it seems like I'm making excuses for her because I don't like jumping to conclusions about people, or thinking the worst of them without seeing for myself. People used to do that about us all the time when I was growing up.' She looked out of the window and added in an undertone, 'And because at least one of us has got to be on speaking terms with her when we get there or it's going to be a very, very awkward evening.'

Villa Luana was a little way out of the village, set into the hillside, surrounded by olive trees and cypresses and pines that perfumed the warm air with their dry, resinous scent. Like Alnburgh, there was something fortress-like about its high, narrow-windowed walls and towers, but if Alnburgh had come from some Gothic horror story, Villa Luana was straight out of Arabian Nights.

They drove through a gate and pulled up in a courtyard where the evening shadows gathered in pools of deep indigo. Ornate silver Moorish lanterns lit up walls that were the soft pink of tea roses. A man dressed in the traditional white djellaba appeared through an open doorway and gave a silent half-bow, indicating with a sweeping gesture of his arm that they should go into the house.

Sophie's nerves cranked up several notches, but Kit's stride was utterly nonchalant, vaguely predatory as she followed him into a huge, high-ceilinged room. Several long windows with delicately inlaid surrounds were set into each wall, giving a panoramic view across the hillside.

It was so beautiful that for a moment Sophie forgot to be nervous and walked across to one of the windows with a low gasp of astonishment. In the west the sun appeared through the branches of the trees like a fat, warm apricot, bathing the villa's garden in syrupy light and unfurling ribbons of shadow across velvety lawns and a mirror-still pool. Beyond that lay the mountains—ink-dark and majestic.

'Welcome to Villa Luana.'

The voice came from behind her and, though it was soft, it still made Sophie jump. Automatically she looked at Kit. In the golden evening sun his face looked curiously drained of colour, but his eyes glittered like frosted steel as he looked at his mother.

Slowly Sophie turned to follow his gaze.

The woman who came towards them was small, slender, dark-haired and still very beautiful. For some reason Sophie had expected her to have adopted the Moroccan style of dressing, or an English version of it, but she was dressed in an exquisite black linen shift dress that owed more to the couture houses of Paris than the souks of Marrakech. Her oval face wore an expression of perfect serenity, though as she came closer Sophie could see lines etched into her forehead and around her eyes.

Eyes that were exactly the same silver-grey as Kit's.

She stopped a few feet away from him.

'Kit. It's been such a long time.' Her voice was low, but it vibrated with suppressed emotion. She was gazing at him; hopefully, avidly, as if he held her future in his hands. As if she was afraid he would disappear again.

'Hasn't it?' Kit drawled quietly. 'Almost thirty years, in fact.'

'Yes.' The acid in his tone must have stung her because she turned away sharply, and noticed Sophie for the first time.

'And you're Kit's fiancée.'

'Yes, I'm Sophie. Sophie Greenham.' Perhaps it was nerves that made her go forward and give Juliet a hug instead of just shaking her hand. Or perhaps it was because, despite her incredible poise and elegance, there was something fragile about her, something vulnerable that made Sophie feel the need to compensate for Kit's hostility. 'It's such a pleasure to meet you.'

'And you. A pleasure and a privilege.' Juliet gave Sophie's shoulders a squeeze, and Sophie understood that she was grateful. 'Now, it's such a beautiful evening I thought we could eat on the roof terrace. Philippe will bring us drinks and we can all get to know each other a little better. I want to hear all about the wedding.'

If the view from the reception hall downstairs was beautiful, from the roof terrace on top of the house it was breathtaking: a melting watercolour in tones of ochre, burnt sienna, indigo and gold.

The sun was touching the horizon, painting the dry earth blood red. Kit leaned against the wall, breathing in the scent of pine and thyme and woodsmoke drifting up from the village and waiting for the adrenaline rushing through his veins to subside.

Seeing her again had brought it all back. The bitterness. The resentment. The anger. His jaw ached from clenching his teeth together, literally biting back the torrent of recrimination that swirled around his brain.

He had come here for answers, not to make polite small talk about weddings. Behind him he could hear Sophie keeping up a stream of gentle conversation as she admired the view, the fruit hanging from the lemon trees that stood in pots around the terrace, the piles of silk cushions on the low couches.

He had never loved her more.

Closing his eyes, he let the sound of her sweet, slightly hesitant voice steady him, and felt his hostility ebb. He heard the manservant arrive, glasses clinking together as a tray was set down. His hands, gripping the edge of the wall, were numb again. The sound of a champagne cork made his taut nerves scream.

He wanted nothing more than to gather Sophie into his arms and take her away. Somewhere where he could shut the world out, and forget it all.

'I thought we should have some champagne, as it's a special evening,' Juliet said. Her voice was exactly as he'd remembered it too. Summoning a bland smile, he turned round to face her.

'Thanks, but I'm driving.'

'Oh—no, I'll drive,' Sophie said, her eyes darting from his face, to Juliet, and back again.

'You're not insured. It's fine. I'll just have mineral water.'

Juliet said something to the manservant, who melted away again. Kit looked away from Sophie's anguished face and out over the hillside again.

'I can see why you left Alnburgh,' he said, not bothering to hide the acid in his tone.

'It's certainly warmer here,' Juliet said with a small, uncomfortable laugh. 'But Alnburgh is beautiful too. You've no idea how much I missed it when I first came here.' She stopped short, obviously aware that she had strayed too soon into dangerous territory, and then turned to Sophie. 'But I want to hear all about you. When Kit said he was engaged I was so thrilled. Tell me about yourself—what do you do for a living?'

Sophie took a gulp of champagne and nearly choked on the bubbles. Too late, she realised that Juliet's glass was still untouched and that she was probably supposed to wait for some kind of toast. Luckily the pink dusk hid her blush.

'If I say I'm an actress that makes it sound terribly grand,' she said, awkwardness making the words spill out too quickly. 'I'm not trained, and, apart from a season I did at The Globe earning peanuts for wafting a palm leaf over Cleopatra for two hours a night, I mostly do bit parts in TV and film.'

'How exciting.' Juliet's eyes kept wandering to where Kit stood a little distance away, his massive shoulders silhouetted against the crimson-streaked sky. 'I'm sure you'll get your big break soon.'

'Oh, I don't really want it, to be honest. I don't long for stardom or anything; in fact I'd absolutely hate it. Being an extra was just something that allowed me to earn money and travel and which didn't need a whole lot of exams, but I'd give it up tomorrow if I could.' She giggled and took another gulp of champagne. 'The film I've just done was about vampires and involved getting done up like a specialist hooker every day for six weeks.'

Philippe came back, carrying a huge tray loaded with tiny dishes and a bottle of mineral water, its sides frosted with condensation. He put the tray on the low table between the two cushion-strewn couches. Juliet motioned for Sophie to sit down.

'And what about you, Kit?' Juliet said softly. 'You're in the army?'

Kit came forwards. The last, flaming rays of the sun lit up his scarred face as he sat down on the couch opposite.

'EOD,' he said tersely, dragging a hand across his torn cheek. 'As you can probably tell.'

'I knew anyway. I've followed your career as much as I could. I read about your George Cross in the papers. I was so proud.' She gave a swift, sad smile. 'I have no right, I know that. But you must be, Sophie.'

Caught off guard, her mouth full of some kind of spicy chickpea thing she'd absent-mindedly picked up from one of the bowls in front of her, Sophie could only nod frantically.

'Anyway, a toast to you both,' Juliet said, picking up her untouched glass and holding it aloft so the golden liquid gleamed. 'To your marriage and your future together. May it be joyful and untroubled.'

Kit looked at Sophie as he raised his mineral water. To her shame Sophie's glass was almost empty.

'To all of us,' she said brightly, in an attempt to dispel the tension that crackled in the sultry evening. 'To a happy, untroubled future.'

Juliet took a tiny sip of champagne. Sophie tried very hard not to drain hers.

'So, tell me about the wedding,' Juliet said, putting her glass down again and looking at Sophie. Sophie could see the anguish in her luminous eyes, and understood the meaning of the term 'noblesse oblige': the effort required to keep the façade of gracious courtesy in place. 'Have you set a date?'

She glanced at Kit. He looked distant to the point of boredom but the restless tap of one long finger against the square arm of the couch betrayed his tension. Her heart squeezed with love and longing.

'We haven't even decided what kind of wedding it's going to be or where,' she said quickly. 'I'm not the kind of person who's been fantasising about ivory silk dresses and gigantic cakes since I was old enough to say "wedding planner" so it really cannot be small enough or private enough for me. A deserted beach would be good...' She trailed off, but the silence crouching in the shadows around them threatened to swamp them. Desperately she ploughed on. 'Lots of my friends have had register-office weddings, but they can be a bit...well, soulless. You come out wondering whether you've just witnessed two people pledging to love each other until they die, or applying for planning permission for a house extension.'

Juliet's smile was wistful. 'What about the chapel at Alnburgh?' she said carefully. 'It's tiny, and so beautiful.'

The tension that had been building in the still air cracked. From opposite Kit gave a muted sound of disgust and got to his feet, dragging a hand through his hair before turning to face Juliet. His silver eyes were luminous with anger.

'And unfortunately not licensed for public marriages. And since it turns out I'm not technically a Fitzroy...'

'Oh, Kit...' Juliet stood up too. The expression on her face was almost defiant, but her voice ached with compassion. 'I wondered if you knew. If you'd somehow worked it out.' She looked down, taking a second to regain her composure. 'That's why I wanted to see you. You *are* a Fitzroy. Alnburgh is yours.'

CHAPTER SEVEN

'WHAT the hell are you talking about?'

Through a fog of adrenaline Kit was dimly aware that his hands were bunched into fists at his sides and that his voice pulsed with anger. He didn't care.

'I saw Ralph's solicitor,' he went on, not bothering to stop his lip from curling into a sneer. 'Ralph's will made it very clear I was nothing to do with him, and he had no intention of letting his family estate fall into the hands of *your* bastard son.'

Juliet took a tiny gasping breath. Her eyes were like headlamps, fixed on his, her face pale.

'I thought he might do something like that. It's why I knew I had to get in touch. Ralph wasn't your father, Kit, but...' she took another quick breath '...but his older brother was. Which means it's you, not Jasper, who is the rightful heir of Alnburgh.'

Once, on duty, Kit had been set upon by a gang of insurgents and dragged into a back alley where they'd kicked and punched him repeatedly before he managed to get away. That scene, complete with the taste of blood and acid in his mouth, the pain under his ribs, came vividly back to him now. He turned away, mentally searching for something to hold onto.

'Ralph's older brother...?'

'Leo,' Juliet said quietly. 'Leo Fitzroy.'

Memories shifted and rearranged themselves. A portrait that used to hang in the hall at Alnburgh before it was moved to some less prominent position. A uniform. 'He was in the army,' Kit rasped. 'He died in the Falklands.'

'No.' He heard Juliet sigh. 'No, he didn't. He fought there, and as time passed and he never came back to Alnburgh that was what people assumed. Ralph didn't set them straight. It reflected well on the family, and it explained why there was no funeral.'

Kit rounded on her. 'What was the truth?'

Wrapping her arms around herself, as if for comfort or protection, Juliet moved away from the table with its virtually untouched dishes. 'I don't know where to start.' She gave a shaky laugh. 'Even though I've been rehearsing telling you all this in my head for weeks.'

'Start at the beginning.' From the couch, Sophie spoke. She was sitting very still, her head bent so that Kit couldn't see her face, but her voice was calm and quiet. 'Start with when you met Leo.'

Kit's heart was beating hard. He wanted to go to her, wanted to pull her against him and bury his face in her hair, but he couldn't move. Juliet went over to light a lamp hanging from the wall, the match illuminating her face for a second, clearly showing the lines of age and sorrow etched there.

'I suppose the beginning is when I met Ralph,' she said slowly, moving over to one of the lemon trees, cupping a fruit in the palm of her hand. The light from the lamp threw a circle of gold around them all and cast their shadows on the terrace wall. Kit remembered when Juliet used to come in to say goodnight to him in his turret bedroom at Alnburgh.

'I'd just finished boarding school and was terribly naive and sheltered,' she was saying in the same soft voice he remembered. 'My parents wanted me to go to Switzerland to some kind of finishing school, mostly because they didn't know what else to do with me while they waited for me to find a suitable husband. Then one weekend a friend invited me to go with her to a house party at Alnburgh.' She pulled a face. 'The seat of the Earls of Hawksworth. My mother was delighted.'

On silent feet the manservant, Philippe, returned, impassively loading the plates back onto the tray, topping up glasses, lighting the candles in the lanterns on the table. As he moved away Juliet came to sit down again.

'I fell in love with the place,' she went on, picking up her glass. 'It was the middle of summer and I'd never been anywhere more romantic. And at the centre of it all was Ralph, this laughing, handsome man who seemed to constantly have a bottle of vintage champagne in one hand and a half-naked blonde in the other.' She broke off to take a sip of her drink. 'The party went on for about three days. My parents were furious when I finally went home.' She gave a hollow laugh. 'Until I told them I was engaged.'

Although it was Juliet who was speaking, although she was his mother and he hadn't seen her for almost thirty years, it was Sophie at whom Kit found himself unable to stop looking. Propped on one elbow on the cushioned couch, she was watching Juliet, and her beautiful face was wistful.

'I thought I was in love with him,' Juliet said sadly, 'but really it was the castle, the glamour, the champagne, the freedom. It was just a shame I only realised that when it was too late. When Leo came to the wedding.'

She faltered, and, in one of the gestures of warmth and compassion that came so naturally to her, Sophie reached out and put a hand on Juliet's arm. In that moment the most prominent of the complex emotions churning inside Kit was gratitude. Sophie had taken responsibility for Juliet's feelings, meaning he could absorb the facts of his own painful history without the burden of responding.

It made it…easier.

'It was awful,' Juliet said bleakly. 'He was Ralph's best man and he only arrived on the morning of the wedding, so the first time I set eyes on him was as I walked down the aisle. It was like I recognised him, in some profound part of myself, and I knew, absolutely, that I was marrying the wrong brother.'

Across the table Sophie's eyes met Kit's, and he knew she too was remembering how she had come to Alnburgh as Jasper's pretend girlfriend. For the briefest second a smile passed across her face, but somehow it just made her look sad.

'So...what did you do?' she murmured, looking away again.

Juliet gave an elegant shrug. 'Nothing. I did what any polite, well-brought-up girl would do and I made my vows and said all the right things at the reception and went away on my honeymoon and tried to be a good, proper wife. But it was a disaster. Ralph had never had any intention of giving up the parties and the half-naked blondes, and I found that Alnburgh wasn't so romantic in winter. I thought I'd die of either loneliness or cold.'

In the sultry twilight Sophie pulled her knees up to her chest and hugged them. 'I know the feeling. I was only there for two weeks, but I could think of nothing but how cold I was.' Her eyes found Kit's again, and another jolt of electricity fizzed through him as she added softly, 'Well, *almost* nothing.'

'Go on.' Kit's voice was like gravel as he forced himself to drag his thoughts away from that time, when Sophie's presence at Alnburgh had been like a knife in his side, tormenting and obsessing him.

'Then Leo came home.'

Juliet sighed and let her head fall back. 'If I say it was impossible to stop what happened between us, that sounds like an excuse. But that was how it felt.'

Tell me about it, Kit thought wearily. If he'd been a nicer person he probably would have said it out loud, to let Juliet know that he was every bit as fallible and incapable of resisting temptation as she and Leo had been, but he didn't. Opposite, Sophie leaned her cheek on her knees and looked at Juliet. Desire beat a relentless tattoo through his veins as he remembered how he had finally given up fighting the want, and in one of the castle's ancient, dusty four-poster beds had given in to it…

'We had three weeks before he had to go away again. We swore that would be it—that it was a one-off, a miraculous slice of perfection that would go no further. We made a decision not to write or keep in touch and so…' her voice cracked slightly '…when I discovered I was pregnant there was no way of contacting him.'

For the first time since she'd started speaking Juliet looked at Kit properly, her expression a mixture of apology and helplessness. 'I didn't even know where he was,' she said, almost imploringly. 'By that time he'd been selected for the SAS and everything he did was top secret. I was terrified. I was also horribly sick, which meant Ralph soon guessed I was pregnant. He was…happy. It didn't cross his mind for a second that it couldn't have been his baby.'

'And you didn't think you should tell him?' Kit said tonelessly.

'Of *course* I did. I thought about nothing else. But I was ill, and Leo wasn't there. I didn't know what to do, so I did nothing.'

Philippe had come back, bearing more dishes, which he set down on the table, seemingly oblivious to the currents of tension flowing across it. As he retreated again Sophie felt an urge to escape from the emotional cyclone that seemed to be building in the thick, hot air and follow him back to the kitchen. Where she belonged.

Kit waited until he was gone to speak again. His eyes were

like lasers as he looked across at his mother, his voice dangerously quiet.

'And *how long* did you do nothing for?'

'You were about a year old when Leo came back.' Juliet didn't meet his gaze, busying herself taking the lid off a terracotta tagine and spooning out its fragrant contents. 'It had always been the plan that Leo would take over the running of the castle when he left the army, but everything had changed. Ralph thought you were his. Leo felt he'd already taken his brother's wife, and he couldn't bring himself to take his child and his home as well.'

Her hand shook, so that cous cous spilled over the tabletop. Raising her head, she looked at Kit. 'He gave up Alnburgh without a second thought, but we couldn't give up each other.'

'So you left to be with him.' In the candlelight his face was masklike, only the cuts showing that he was flesh and blood. 'Did you just *forget* to take me with you?'

Sophie's head throbbed. She discovered that she wanted very much to shut her eyes and put her hands over her ears, to make it all go away, like a child.

'Oh, Kit, it wasn't that simple!' For the first time Juliet's voice lost its careful moderation and became raw with weary emotion. 'I didn't leave straight away, as you know. We *tried* to stop seeing each other, but deep down we both knew it was hopeless, and in the end we stopped feeling guilty. He was abroad a lot—places I read about in the newspapers, places that were synonymous with violence and terror—and the whole thing had an air of tempting fate about it. He'd survived another tour, another siege, another shoot-out and he came back to me to celebrate being alive.'

Kit flinched.

'But after the Falklands it was different. Leo changed. He couldn't do it any more. He'd been posted in Gibraltar for a time, and that was when he'd bought this place, to come to when he had time, to relax. He wanted to come and live here full time, and he wanted us to join him—*both* of us.'

For a moment Kit said nothing. Somewhere in the distance a dog barked.

'So what happened?'

Sophie heard Juliet take a breath, as if she was steadying herself. Or preparing herself for something.

'He wasn't well when he came back from the Falklands. He wasn't sleeping, and he'd noticed things—things he assumed would get better when he got back here and had a chance to rest. When they didn't he came back to London to get checked out.'

Kit stood up abruptly, raising his hands to his temples. Stumbling to her feet, Sophie saw that they were clenched into fists.

'Go *on*.'

He spoke through gritted teeth, and when Sophie touched him he didn't seem to notice her.

'He got passed around a few specialists—different addresses on Harley Street who each subjected him to a battery of tests before referring him on to the next doctor.' Juliet's voice was eerily calm again now. 'I wasn't with him when he went to the last one. A neurologist. The one who told him he was suffering from a progressive illness affecting the central nervous system, and that he had a year to live.'

Kit turned away, walking over to the edge of the terrace as Juliet continued. The ache in Sophie's head had been joined by a burning feeling in her chest.

'It's a marvellous way of focusing your mind, hearing something like that. Suddenly everything seemed simple.'

'Leaving your child seemed *simple*?' Kit asked hollowly. It was dark now, and the magnificent view was swallowed up by layers of shadow. Beyond the circle of light on the terrace there was nothing to see, but he stared out into the blackness anyway, until his eyes stung.

'A year.' From behind him Juliet sounded very tired. 'I thought that was all. And I couldn't take you halfway across the world to be with a man you barely knew, a man who was terminally ill and was going to need me twenty-four hours a day. You needed school, routine...'

I needed parents, Kit thought bleakly. He'd needed *her*. But with a crushing sensation in his chest he could see that Leo had needed her too. His father. He had needed her more.

'So why didn't you come back?' he said harshly.

She sighed, a long, sad sigh. 'Because the doctors were wrong. They told us what would happen, how his body would shut down, bit by bit, like lights being switched off, until he couldn't move, couldn't swallow, couldn't breathe. They were right about that, but what they badly underestimated was how long it would take.'

Slowly Kit turned round.

'How long?'

'Sixteen years. He lived for sixteen years. So you see, by then it was far too late to come back.'

Looking back later, Sophie could remember very little of the evening after that. She wasn't really aware of what they ate, only that it was delicious enough for her to find that her plate was empty, and she was hungry enough to accept a second helping. Her glass seemed to empty itself very quickly, and be filled again by invisible hands. The warm air caressed her and Juliet's low, musical voice lulled her, distracting her from the dark shapes that moved in the back of her mind.

She talked of safe things. Of the labour of love that had been the restoration of Villa Luana, the way Leo had gradually won the trust and respect of the local people. Kit said little, and with the candlelight flickering over his face he looked like a carved saint in church: silent and suffering.

It was as if the hurricane had passed and they had emerged into a calmer place. But the damage had still been done.

Sophie was too tired, too overwhelmed by the revelations of the evening to think about what that damage might be.

'You've made a very good choice.'

Juliet's voice was gentle as she looked down at Sophie, fast asleep on her nest of cushions. Her hair was spread out over the vibrant-coloured silk, and in the warm lantern-glow it was every bit as rich and precious and gleaming. She looked like an Eastern princess in some exotic tale.

'Yes.' Kit's throat was tight with emotion. With love, and despair, and fear.

'Although really, you don't choose who you fall in love with,' Juliet said. 'When it happens, that's it. And it doesn't matter how impossible it is, you can't change it because you know you're in for good. For life.'

Kit made a hollow sound that wasn't quite a laugh. A pulse beat painfully in his temples, as if everything that he'd discovered that evening was gathered there. 'It's not always that straightforward though, is it? You can't always just go with it because you *want* to.'

He spoke more angrily than he'd meant to, and realised that she would think he was talking about her and Leo and the small boy they'd left behind. He wasn't. He was thinking of himself as an adult. Now. Himself and Sophie and their future, which seemed suddenly fragile in the light of the things Juliet had just told him.

Sophie stirred. A frown appeared for a second between her eyebrows and she raised her hands to cover her ears, as if she had heard his outburst and was blocking it out. Kit tensed against the tidal wave of love that crashed through him, the swell of cold, churning panic that followed in its wake.

Juliet waited until she was still again. 'I understand that you're angry with me,' she said, very softly. 'I don't expect anything else. But I'm so glad that you came and gave me a chance to explain. Even if you can't forgive what happened, I wanted to make sure you knew about Alnburgh.'

She got to her feet, glancing at Sophie again. 'Let's not wake her. Come downstairs—I've had a copy made of Leo's will for you. All the details about the estate are in there.'

Kit stood up and went over to Sophie, looking down at her, fighting the urge to bend and kiss her slightly parted lips. In the constantly changing landscape of his life she was the one thing that was the same, the one thing that was true and good and wholly beautiful, *but*…

He tore his gaze away from her and forced himself to follow Juliet.

'The details being?' he asked blandly. The palms of his hands were burning. He didn't care about the estate. There were other things he needed her to tell him.

'It was all sorted out legally at the point when we got divorced. Leo forfeited his right to inherit Alnburgh. He figured it was a bargain—he got me, and Ralph got the estate and an heir.'

The stairs from the roof terrace emerged onto a galleried landing over the central hallway below. Lamplight illuminated the intricate plaster friezes and carved doors, the metal grille of an old-fashioned lift. Kit followed her along the landing and into a large room. She flicked a switch and the huge metalwork lantern hanging from the high ceiling lit up a sparsely furnished space, containing only a chest of drawers, a dressing table and a narrow single bed.

Kit's heart felt a jolt as he noticed the silver dressing-table set—hairbrush, mirror and tortoiseshell comb—he remembered from his mother's bedroom at Alnburgh.

'So Leo effectively signed away his son to his brother?'

Juliet went over to the chest of drawers and pulled open the top drawer. 'He was ill by then. He knew he couldn't be a proper father, although he wanted to…*so much*. Making sure the legal agreement was watertight and Alnburgh was yours was the one thing he could do.'

She turned round slowly and Kit saw that she was holding a sheaf of photographs.

'It was very brutal, his illness.' There was a break in her voice as she held out the photographs. 'He was such a strong, powerful man.'

Kit felt as if something were wrapped tightly around his throat. The top photo was of Leo Fitzroy in camouflage uniform, squinting against the sun, half turned towards the camera. The background was the featureless beige of a desert, and Kit could almost feel the heat, picture him walking away, continuing to issue orders to the men who were just out of shot.

'You're so like him.'

It was true. He could see that for himself. He looked at the next photograph. Leo in civilian clothes this time, his arm around Juliet in some pavement café, glasses of Pernod and postcards on the tin table in front of them. It was the Juliet Kit remembered, young and smiling. The mother Leo had taken.

'Marbella,' she said softly. 'I was writing you a postcard.'

And so it went on. Pictures of a thinner Leo standing outside Villa Luana, with a gin and tonic in his hand on the roof terrace, in a wheelchair.

Kit's hand was shaking as he continued to the last photograph. It was a close-up of Leo, skeletal now, propped up against a mountain of pillows, a breathing tube in his neck. His cheeks were sunken, his wasted hands resting impassively on the sheets.

'The doctors were right about what the disease would do to him,' Juliet said huskily. 'As you can see, it ravaged his body completely, without mercy. But it didn't touch the man I loved inside.'

Kit found he was looking into the eyes of the man in the

photo. His father. His face was slack and expressionless, but his eyes were bright, alive, full of love.

'That was the cruellest thing,' Juliet went on. 'But it was also the most wonderful. And although the price I paid to be with him was *so high*…' She faltered, pressing a hand to her lips for a moment. 'Every day we had together was a blessing.'

Kit gave the photos back to her. He had the same feeling he got in the aftermath of an explosion, when all the oxygen had been sucked from the air and his lungs were full of grit. His hands felt as if they'd been crushed by boulders.

'This illness…' he said hoarsely, taking a few steps away from her. Suddenly he understood the reason for the single bed, and the lift he'd noticed on the landing, and felt faint.

'Motor Neurone Disease.' Juliet sighed. 'Sadly it's not that rare.'

Kit swung round to look at her again. Blood was pounding in his ears.

'Is it hereditary?'

She turned away, shuffling the photos into a neat stack in her hands as she took them back to the drawer again. Seconds ticked by.

'No,' she said, without looking at him. 'Almost always not.'

Another explosion ripped through Kit's head. He could feel the sweat gathering in the small of his back.

'What does that mean?'

Juliet was looking through the contents of the drawer, her head bent. 'We asked the specialist. In maybe ten per cent of cases, I think there might be a genetic link, but for the vast majority it's just chance. Here—'

She came back over to him, holding out a large Manila envelope and, on top of it, a square velvet box. Kit stared at it without registering.

Ten per cent. One in ten cases…

'It's Leo's will,' Juliet prompted. 'You might want your own copy. And this…' she held out the velvet box '…is the Fitzroy ring. The Dark Star. I couldn't help noticing that Sophie doesn't have an engagement ring yet. Perhaps—'

A sinister voice inside Kit's head told him not to take it. That giving it to Sophie would be like shackling her to him with a ball and chain. But somehow he found himself holding the box in his hand.

'It's late. We should go.'

Juliet nodded, then reached up to take hold of his shoulders. 'Thank you,' she said fiercely. 'I'm so very, very glad you came.'

Kit leaned down, kissing her briefly on the cheek, wishing he could say the same.

CHAPTER EIGHT

As Sophie swam slowly into consciousness the first thing she was aware of was that her head hurt. The second was that the uneasy feeling somewhere in the pit of her stomach was only partly the result of too much champagne the night before.

She opened her eyes. Through the fretwork shutters the sky was a clear delphinium blue. Beside her the bed was empty.

Kit was always up ages before her. It didn't mean anything was wrong, she told herself, sitting up and putting a hand up to her aching head. Looking down, she saw that she was still wearing last night's silk tunic.

She let out a moan of dismay.

Oh, God, she'd fallen asleep, hadn't she? The last thing she remembered was sitting on Juliet Fitzroy's elegant terrace…the champagne, the warm night, her beautiful voice with its impeccable English accent telling the story of how she'd fallen in love with Leo. And dropping the bombshell that Kit was still a Fitzroy and heir of Alnburgh.

Falling back onto the bed, she pulled the pillow over her head.

There were other, slightly more hazy memories. Kit carrying her down to the car, and how being held against him had made her feel safe again, though safe from what she wasn't quite so sure. She remembered twining her arms around his neck as he'd lowered her into the seat, and how he'd detached her with a finality that felt like rejection.

Oh, dear. She had some apologising to do.

Carefully she got to her feet. Being upright wasn't as bad as she'd feared, and once her head had stopped protesting at the movement she tugged her top down and went in search of water, and Kit.

She found him out on the terrace. He was wearing last night's trousers and no shirt, and the sight of his broad, muscular back, already the colour of sun-baked terracotta, made her completely forget her hangover. Going up to him, she slid her arms around his neck and pressed her lips to the warm skin between his shoulder blades.

'If I've missed breakfast is there any chance I could just have you instead?' she murmured huskily.

He went very still. Somehow, Sophie found that more unsettling than if he'd pulled away.

'You haven't missed breakfast,' he said neutrally, putting down the sheaf of papers he'd been reading. 'I'll get something sent up now.'

Sophie stood up and stepped back. She felt slightly sick, but couldn't be sure if it was her hangover or Kit's chilling indifference. Welcome to Planet Paranoia, she sneered silently at herself, going round to the front of his chair and sitting down on the one opposite. From the front he looked even more gorgeous. He was wearing dark glasses and his hair was standing on end where he'd run his fingers through it. The bottom half of his face beneath the scars, which were healing nicely now, was shadowed with stubble.

'I'm sorry about last night,' she said ruefully. 'And to be honest I'm not that hungry. I really would just rather have you.'

'There are some things I need to do. I'm still going through this.'

He held up the sheaf of papers. Sophie could see her own

face reflected in the lenses of his sunglasses. Pale. Needy. She aimed for interested and supportive instead.

'Oh? What is it?'

'Leo's will.'

Acid churned in her stomach and the smile faded from her face. 'Ah. Yes. That was a bit of a bombshell, wasn't it? So, it turns out Alnburgh is yours after all.' She laughed uneasily. 'Jasper will be over the moon.'

'I'll need to see him when we get home.'

He seemed to have surrounded himself with some kind of invisible, impenetrable force field. Sophie swallowed back the acid fear that was rising in her throat as she mentally ran through the possible reasons for it.

'Well, he's in LA at the moment,' she said as lightly as she could. 'Once he hears he's off the hook he'll probably throw a party of such epic proportions that he'll still be recovering by Christmas.' She broke off, realising that she might not be in the best position to criticise on that score. Moistening her dry lips and pleating the embroidered hem of the silk tunic with shaky fingers, she quickly changed tack. 'What about you…? How do you feel about it all? You must be happy to find that you're a Fitzroy after all.' She managed a smile. 'And not just *any* Fitzroy, but the one who gets to inherit everything…'

He laughed then. Which, since it had been meant as a joke, was good. But it was a sound of such hollow bitterness that Sophie felt her insides freeze.

'*Happy?* Not exactly. Believe me, inheriting *everything* is a very mixed blessing.'

She got to her feet, clammy with nausea. She understood his meaning. Being the Earl of Hawksworth brought with it responsibilities, one of which was undoubtedly making a suitable marriage to a woman who had what it took to carry off a tiara and a title, and fulfil the duty of providing further heirs.

Everything she had joked about with Jasper over lunch the other day when this had been impossible enough to joke about. Everything she wasn't and couldn't ever be.

Kit lifted a hand to his forehead, rubbing his long, strong fingers across it as if trying to erase something. 'I have some calls to make.'

'I'll go and have a shower,' Sophie muttered, backing towards the door.

'I think I'm going to need to get back today,' Kit continued, without looking up. 'I'll get Nick to fly me to Newcastle and hire a car to Alnburgh.'

Sophie stopped. 'What about me?'

Kit raised his head, but he didn't turn to look at her.

'I know how you feel about Alnburgh,' he said in a voice of great weariness. 'I don't expect you to come if you don't want to. But you must understand that I have to go.'

A tiny spark of hope glowed in the darkness of Sophie's misery. Or it could have been a spark of desperation. Either way he hadn't told her that he didn't want her there.

'I do want to.' She swallowed hard, raising her chin and forcing herself to smile as she looked at him. 'Alnburgh might not be top of my dream destination list but you've just been away for five months. I'm not ready to let you go again so soon. I want to come with you.'

Kit waited until he'd heard the distant sound of the bathroom door shutting before expelling the breath he'd been holding and dropping Leo's will onto the table.

He hadn't quite been telling the truth when he'd said he was still going through it. He'd been up all night, ploughing through pages of dense legal jargon that effectively restored his birthright, and it was clear enough. Just as Juliet had explained, Leo might have been denied an active role as a father, but he had spared no effort to make sure he passed on Alnburgh to his son.

Sophie was right, he should be delighted. Instead he could only think of what else Leo might have passed on to him.

He checked his watch. The doctors in the military medical unit should have done their rounds by now, so it was a good time to ring to see how Lewis was. It might also be possible to talk to Randall. They'd served together and Kit trusted him. Randall would give him a straight answer about whether the numbness in his hands, the pins and needles in his fingers, were the first signs of the disease that had slowly crucified his unknown father.

Kit picked up his phone and scrolled through his contacts until he found the number. Whether he could deal with that answer was another issue altogether.

Sophie got out of the shower and buried her face in a towel that was as thick and soft as a duvet. Ten minutes under powerful jets of steaming water had done little for her hangover and even less for her sense of dread, particularly as fragmented memories from last night were coming back thick and fast now.

'You're as good as anyone else.' That had been her mother's mantra when Sophie was growing up, but Rainbow had obviously never spent an evening with someone as poised and graceful and dignified as Juliet Fitzroy. Sophie's groan of dismay was muffled by the towel as she remembered gulping champagne, swamping Juliet in an inelegant hug the moment she met her, chattering inanely about her flaky job—oh, God, had she really used the phrase 'specialist hooker'?—and—the final disgrace—falling asleep the moment dinner was over.

She didn't blame Kit if he was doubting the wisdom of his impulsive proposal.

Going through to the bedroom, she could hear the low murmur of his voice as he spoke into his mobile, but although she strained to hear it was impossible to make out what he was saying. The white dress she'd worn yesterday was thrown over a chair and she picked it up, sliding it quickly over her head because she lacked the energy to find anything else. Through the intricate shutters she could see him, standing at the far end of the terrace where he must have gone deliberately to place himself out of earshot. His back was towards her, but he was standing as if tensed to fight.

She leaned her head against the shutters for a moment, remembering how she'd once told him that she wanted a man who would fight for her. And he had. When they'd almost been pulled apart by circumstances and misunderstandings he'd looked beyond the evidence of his own eyes and the prejudices of others and he'd come to find her, and fight for her.

Would he do it again?

One thing Sophie had learned from her free-spirited mother was that you couldn't force love, or keep it in a cage. If she was going to be with Kit, sharing the life that had now been thrust upon him, it had to be because he wanted her there, not because he was honouring a promise made under different circumstances.

She wasn't prepared to let him go without trying, she acknowledged sadly, but she had to give him space to get to grips with this new development.

Hastily she took a pad of hotel paper from beside the bed and scrawled a note. Then, slipping on her sandals and grabbing her bag, she let herself quietly out.

'So, what does that mean? That he's going to be all right?'

The shooting pains down Kit's forearm told him he was probably holding the phone too tightly as he listened to Randall's update on Lewis, but his hand was so numb he was afraid of dropping his mobile entirely if he loosened his grip. He stared out into the blue haze over the rooftops of the city, but in his mind he was back in that corridor outside Lewis's room, strangled by guilt.

'It means that there doesn't seem to be any permanent

damage to his spinal cord,' Randall said smoothly. 'It was a bloody close thing, but the bullet seems to have missed it by a millimetre or so. Of course, he's got a long way to go before he's up and about, but at least it does look like that day will eventually come.'

'Thank God for that.'

'Indeed,' Randall said wryly. 'But how are you, Kit? I know it wasn't the easiest of tours.'

'I'm fine,' Kit said curtly. 'I was actually wearing a bomb suit for once, or else I wouldn't be here. I got a few cuts on my face because the visor was up, but they're healing OK.'

'I'm pleased to hear it, but I'm not sure you've answered my question,' Randall remarked gently. 'I know you walked away from the explosion largely unscathed but I meant, how are you in yourself?'

'All right. Just need to catch up on some sleep, that's all.'

He closed his eyes, inwardly cursing as his courage failed him. He wanted to know, and yet he couldn't bring himself to ask. God, what a coward.

Perhaps Randall sensed something in the sharpness of his voice because he persisted.

'Not sleeping well?'

'I never sleep well. But after being away for five months there always seem to be more pressing things to do in bed.'

Randall laughed. 'In that case you only have yourself to blame.'

That was as far as he was going to press it, and Kit could tell by the tone of his voice that he was about to say goodbye and hang up. Suddenly his blood was pounding, his palms slick with sweat. He took a breath in.

'Before you go, how much do you know about Motor Neurone Disease?'

There was a moment's silence. 'Well, I'm not a specialist. Was there anything specific you wanted to know?'

'Yes. What are the early symptoms?'

From the other end of the line he heard Randall expel a long, heavy breath. 'I don't know, Kit. Every case is different, but muscle weakness in the hands or feet, I guess—probably more noticeably in the hands—clumsiness, lack of co-ordination, that kind of thing. Why?'

Kit ignored the question, his mind spooling back to those long moments beneath the bridge when his fingers had fumbled helplessly with the wire cutters.

'What treatments are there?'

'There's no cure, if that's what you mean,' Randall said reluctantly. 'Progress of the disease can be slowed slightly with drugs. It's not pretty.'

'No. I know that.'

'But those symptoms are common to a huge number of illnesses that are a lot less serious and a lot more common,' Randall continued, adopting a self-consciously cheerful tone. 'MND really would be a worst case scenario, and a pretty unlikely one at that.'

Unless there was a genetic predisposition, thought Kit hollowly.

'Kit? Are you still there? Look, why don't you come in and see me when you get back? It would give Lewis a boost to have a visit from his commanding officer and I could give you a quick once-over if there's anything that you're worried about.'

'No. There's no need. Really.'

Wing Commander Mike Randall had been an army medic for long enough to know that soldiers responded to questions from a doctor in the same way they would to enemy torture—with stony refusal to co-operate. A more subtle approach was often needed. 'How about a game of squash? It's a while since we've played, although that could be because you always win. Fancy thrashing me again?'

Kit understood exactly what Randall was doing, and in

some distant, dispassionate quarter of his brain he appreciated it.

'I'd love to, but…' he lifted the hand that wasn't holding the phone and held it out in front of him, stretching out his fingers as far as he could until the ache in his tendons just about dispelled the tingling numbness '…some things have come up. Family business. I'm going to be in Northumberland for the next few weeks.'

'OK, Kit. I get the picture.' Randall gave a rueful sigh. 'But I'm here if you need me. If there's anything else you want to ask.'

'Thanks, but you've answered everything already,' Kit said neutrally. 'Lewis needs you, not me. Give him my regards.'

Ending the call, he turned away from the city spread out beneath him and tossed his phone down on the low table. A band of pain across his shoulders told him he'd spent the duration of that entire conversation with every muscle in his body tensed, ready to fight.

Even though there was no point. The enemy he faced couldn't be beaten.

With a thud of alarm he realised that Sophie must be out of the shower by now, and wondered if she'd heard any of that. Quickly he crossed the sun-baked terrace and went inside.

It was cool and dim. And quiet. In the bedroom a note lay on the chest of drawers.

Gone to medina to buy postcard for Jasper. See you later. Love S x

Relief that she hadn't heard poured through him. He could carry on as normal, pretend that everything was all right. If he didn't go and see Randall, or get any kind of formal diagnosis, that meant he wasn't lying to her.

But there was a whole lot of difference between not lying

to her and knowingly trapping her into a marriage that would make her a prisoner.

The ring Juliet had given him was still in the pocket of his trousers and he took it out now, flipping open the lid of the velvet box. The stone was called a black opal, although against the midnight satin lining of the box it glowed with a kaleidoscope of shifting colours, lit up by the diamonds that encircled it.

He stared at it for a long time. Then, shutting the box with a snap, he put it back in his pocket and went out to find her.

The car from the hotel dropped him by the square. Heading towards the medina in the blast-furnace heat, he took the mobile phone from his pocket and brought up Sophie's number. He kept his head down, pressing the phone against his ear and concentrating on its steady ring instead of the cacophony of street vendors and musicians and a thousand conversations around him.

Come on, Sophie, pick up...

The narrow streets of the medina were dark and cool. It was a relief to be out of the sun, but the shadows crawled with menace. He could feel the sheen of sweat covering every inch of his skin, making his shirt stick to him. He quickened his pace so that he was almost running, pushing through the ambling crowds of people as his gaze darted around, looking for a red head amongst the dark or covered ones.

Why wasn't she answering her phone?

His heartbeat reverberated through his body as he scanned the street, his training kicking in automatically as he checked for suspicious signs. There were scores of them—bags of rubbish left in doorways, people wearing layers of clothing that could conceal explosives, carrying bags and packages of every shape and size and muttering to themselves as they walked. *Just like in any busy city street the world over*, mocked a voice of scornful rationality inside Kit's head.

Ahead of him he could see the arched gateway of the souk, leading out onto the wide street beyond. And in front of it, her hair gleaming in a narrow shaft of sunlight filtering through the blinds above, he saw Sophie.

She was sitting on a low stool facing a heavily veiled woman who held one of her hands. The air left Kit's lungs in a rush of relief. Resisting the urge to break into a run and haul her into his arms, he slowed right down, taking a deep breath in and expelling it again in an effort to steady his racing pulse. She was having a henna tattoo—that was why she couldn't answer her phone. Not because she'd been kidnapped, or dragged into a back alley by a gang of thugs, for pity's sake. His scalp prickled with sweat as he raked a hand through his hair and started towards her again.

And stopped.

In a doorway opposite a man was holding a mobile phone. As if in slow motion Kit watched him begin to press buttons on the keypad.

Adrenaline, like neat, iced alcohol, sluiced through his veins, sending his heart-rate into overdrive. Instantly his whole body was rigid, primed, as he reached for his gun. Instead he found himself clutching his phone again, but his fingers were shaking so badly that he dropped it.

As if in slow motion he watched it fall to the ground. He knew he had to reach Sophie before the blast but was suddenly paralysed, his feet rooted to the spot where he stood as horror solidified like concrete in his chest and dark spots danced before his eyes. His mouth was open to shout her name but his throat was tight and dry and could produce no sound.

But it was as if she heard him anyway because at that moment she lifted her head and looked round, straight towards where he stood. The smile died on her face and she got to her feet, coming towards him with her arms outstretched.

'Kit! Kit—what is it?'

The compassion in her voice hit him like acid in the face, bringing him back to reality and turning his panic into self-disgust in a lurching heartbeat. Reaching him, she raised her hand to his cheek, stroking her thumb gently over the half-healed scars there.

'Sweetheart, what's wrong?'

Behind her the man was speaking into his mobile phone now, his face impassive. Kit jerked his head away from Sophie's touch as if it burned him.

'Nothing. Nothing's wrong,' he said in a voice that was as cold and hard as steel. 'I came to find you because I've arranged the flight for one o'clock. We need to pack and get to the airport—if you still want to come back with me.'

Sophie dropped her hand, its intricate henna markings still glistening wetly, and took a step backwards. Dropping her gaze, she nodded.

'Yes. Of course I do.'

Knives of self-loathing pierced him, but still pride prevented him from taking her hand. From apologising, or explaining. Instead he turned on his heel and began to walk back along the street, keeping his gaze fixed unwaveringly ahead.

CHAPTER NINE

THE flight back to England was every bit as luxurious as the one they had taken two days previously, but considerably less enjoyable.

Neither of them spoke much. Kit seemed to have placed himself behind a wall of glass, so that even though he was only a few feet away from her, Sophie felt as if he were somewhere far beyond her reach. Sitting in the deep embrace of the huge seat, she stared out of the window, longing to cross the small distance between them and tear the paperwork out of his hand and force him to notice her, to *talk* to her...

To tell her exactly what had been going through his mind when she'd seen him in the souk earlier, and what had made him look like a man who was being crucified by his own conscience?

But she had a sickening fear that if she did there would be no going back, because the things he told her would change everything. How could she wilfully bring about her own expulsion from the paradise she had allowed herself to believe was hers for ever?

It was early evening when they reached Alnburgh. Even in the height of an English summer, the contrast with the heat and the rich colours of Morocco couldn't have been starker. Carved from iron-grey stone, it appeared to rise straight up out of the cliffs above a stretch of windswept beach, and for miles it had loomed on the horizon, managing to look far more menacing than the Disneyesque castle in the Romanian pine forest where the vampire movie had been filmed.

Sophie's spirits sank even further.

She remembered the first time she'd seen it. It had been a winter night, in the middle of a blizzard, and with its floodlights switched on Alnburgh Castle had looked just like a child's snowglobe. She'd been enchanted, but that was before she'd realised it was just as cold inside as it was outside.

'I can see why Tatiana couldn't wait to move to London the moment Ralph's funeral was over,' she said with a shiver. 'It's not exactly cosy, is it? Are any of the staff still there?'

'Not as far as I know,' said Kit. His voice was gravelly with misuse, and more sexy than ever. 'Obviously Tatiana didn't want to pay them to stay on if she wasn't living there—not when she's haemorrhaging cash to live in a suite at Claridges while she has the London house vandalised by her interior decorator.'

Sophie pressed the button to activate the car heater, and directed the jet of warm air onto her icy feet. She was still wearing the little gold flip-flops, which were covered in pink Marrakech dust. They were already driving under the clock tower, but she knew from previous experience that this might be the last opportunity she had to be warm for a long time.

'It's a big responsibility, isn't it?' she said faintly, wondering if now was the time to ask how quickly he could sort things out so they could get back to London.

'Yes.'

Kit brought the car to a standstill and cut the engine. In the sudden quiet she could hear the muffled sound of the sea and the plaintive crying of gulls.

'Sophie, I know this isn't what you wanted, or expected…'

Ever since she'd followed him through the souk in Marrakech Sophie had been desperate for him to make some move to bridge the terrible chasm that seemed to have opened up between them, but the note of weary resignation in his voice now made her insides freeze. They'd come all this way, he'd delivered her back to England, so was this the start of the 'it's never going to work' speech? In the soft, pastel-coloured evening light he looked beautiful and exhausted and so remote it was as if he had already left her. She could feel the blood draining from her head, leaving a vacuum of airless panic.

'I know, but to be fair you hardly expected it either,' she said, reaching for the door handle, prising it open with shaky fingers. 'Gosh, look how long the grass is. Don't you feel a bit like Robin Hood returning from the crusades?'

She stumbled out of the car, grabbing the carrier bag of duty-free stuff she'd bought while he'd been sorting out the hire car—two bottles of champagne, some uber-fashionable vodka in a neon-pink bottle and a giant Toblerone for Jasper. Taking in a deep lungful of salty air, she wrapped her arms around her as the sea breeze sliced straight through the flimsy white dress. The denim jacket she'd put on over it was completely inadequate for keeping out the chill of the Northumberland evening. Or that of Kit's distance.

Behind her she heard Kit's door slam.

'Do you have keys?' she asked, turning to follow him up the steps to the giant-sized front door.

'Don't need them.' He tapped some numbers into a discreet keypad. 'Tatiana made my f—Ralph—have an electronic system installed.' The door creaked heavily open. 'After you.'

Sophie remembered the armoury hall very well from her first visit. By Alnburgh standards it was a small room, but every inch of the high stone walls was covered with hundreds of swords, pistols, shields and sinister-looking daggers hung in intricate patterns. She'd been deeply intimidated by it the first time, and, standing in the middle of the stone floor and looking around, she didn't feel much better now.

'Home sweet home,' she said with an attempt at humour.

'The first thing I think we should do is take all these awful guns and things down and put up some coat hooks and a nice mirror. Much more welcoming, and practical.'

Gathering up the thick drift of envelopes from the floor, Kit didn't smile. Sophie decided she'd better shut up. Jokes like that, coming from the girl who grew up on a converted bus, were clearly too close to the bone to be funny.

'Just going to the loo,' she muttered, walking into the long gallery where the heads of various kinds of deer and antelope slaughtered by past Fitzroys glared down through the half-light. Until she'd come here, if someone had said 'stuffed animal' to her it would have conjured up an image of cuddly teddy bears, she thought miserably. The scent of woodsmoke hung in the air, a whispered memory of past warmth that couldn't quite mask the unmistakable smell of damp.

In the portrait hall, from which the wide staircase curved upwards, Sophie came face to face with Jasper's mother. Or the seven-foot-high painted version of her anyway, which was every bit as intimidating and glamorous as the real thing. She paused in front of it, looking up. The painter, whoever he was, had captured Tatiana's fine-boned, Slavic beauty, and the quietly triumphant expression in the blue eyes that seemed, quite literally, to look down on Sophie. The diamonds that glittered at her throat, ears and wrist sent out sharp points of painted white, which really did seem to light up the fading evening light.

Sophie sighed. She was completely unable to imagine herself in a similar portrait, decked out in satin and dripping with diamonds. Moving away quickly, she went up the stairs. When she'd first arrived at Alnburgh the labyrinthine passageways upstairs had completely confused her, but at least now she knew where to find a bathroom. Unlike the staterooms downstairs, upstairs had escaped the attentions of Tatiana's interior designer and the chilly corridors were suffused with the breath of age and neglect. The bathroom Sophie went into had last been updated in the nineteen thirties and featured an enormous cast-iron bath standing on lion's feet and pea-green rectangular tiles laid like brickwork. It was refrigerator-cold.

There was no loo paper, but luckily Sophie found the tattered remains of her paper napkin from the aeroplane in her pocket and sent silent thanks to Nick McAllister. She had just pulled the clanking chain and was about to go out again when something on the floor by the door caught her eye and stopped her in her tracks.

Her scream bounced off the tiled walls and echoed along the winding passageways.

Downstairs, Kit froze.

Instinct took over. In a split second he was sprinting up the stairs, taking them two at a time, adrenaline sluicing through his veins like acid. In that instant he was back on duty, his mind racing ahead, anticipating broken bodies, blood, fear and calculating what resources he had to deal with them. Tearing along the corridor, he saw the bathroom door was ajar and kicked it open.

'Sophie...'

There was no blood. Heart pounding, that was what he registered first. And when he'd processed that fact he noticed that she was standing squeezed into the narrow space between the bath and the toilet, her clenched fists clasped beneath her chin, her whole body hunched up in an attitude of utter terror.

'Don't move!' she croaked.

He stopped dead. Reality swung dizzily away from him for a second and he was back in the desert. Images of mines half covered with earth flashed through his head.

Slowly, her eyes round with terror, Sophie unfurled one arm and pointed to the floor just to one side of him.

'There.'

He turned his head, looked down. Blinked.

'A spider,' he rasped. 'It's just a *spider*.'

'*Just* a spider? It's not *just* anything! It's massive. Please, Kit,' she sobbed, 'I *hate* them. Please…*get rid* of it.'

In one swift movement he swooped down to capture it, but his stiff fingers refused to co-operate and it darted away. Sophie screamed again, shrinking back against the wall as it shot towards her.

This time he got it. Somehow he closed his tingling fingers around it, and then, throwing open the badly fitting window, let it go.

'Is it gone?'

He showed her his empty hand. Residual adrenaline still coursed through him, making it impossible to speak, even if he'd trusted himself. His breathing was fast and ragged. He turned away, pressing his fingers to his temples, trying to hold back his anger.

'Thank you,' Sophie said shakily from behind him. 'I can't bear them. We used to get really huge ones—like that—on the bus and Rainbow always insisted they had as much right as we did to be there and wouldn't touch them. I used to lie in bed…*t-terrified* and imagining them crawling under my bedclothes—'

Her voice broke into a hiccupping sob and she put a hand, with its incongruous henna tattoo, to her mouth to stifle it.

She was always so strong and funny and positive, but seeing her pressed against the grim tiles, her bravado in tatters and the tears beginning to slide down her cheeks, Kit felt his resolve crack. In one step he was beside her, pulling her forwards and into his arms, covering her trembling mouth with his.

'It's OK. You're safe now. It's gone.'

It was so good to hold her, so *good* to kiss her again. The relentless nightmare of the last twenty-four hours faded as he breathed in her warm, musky scent and felt her heart thudding frantically against his chest. His hands cupped her face, and in some distant part of his brain he was aware that the numbness and the pins-and-needles sensation was completely gone. He could feel the heat of her cheeks, her velvet skin, each tear that ran across the back of his hand.

The realisation severed the last thread of his reserve. The desire that had been smouldering dangerously during the long journey when she'd slept beside him, her head falling onto his shoulder, mushroomed into a fireball. And as always, her need matched his. Her hands moved downwards, over his chest, pulling at his shirt.

'Not here,' he growled, pulling away.

She gave a gasp of laughter. Her cheeks were damp and flushed, her eyes glittering with arousal. 'I'm glad you said that. After seeing that monster spider I don't want to get down on the floor.'

'Come on.'

Taking her hand, he pulled her forwards, through the gloomy corridors of the castle, up a flight of stone spiral stairs. Her feet caught in the long hem of her white dress and she stumbled. His grip on her hand tightened reflexively, stopping her from falling, and with the other hand he hauled her against him. Sophie could feel the hardness of his erection and gave a moan of need. Their eyes met.

'Where are we going?'

They were both breathing in rapid rasps.

'My room. *Our* room.'

'Is it far? Because I…'

She trailed off, breathless, and he stooped down and scooped her up into his arms, striding up the remaining steps. Freed from the need to look where she was going, Sophie was able to focus her full attention on kissing him, starting at the angle of his jaw, moving upwards to take his ear lobe between her teeth, breathing out gently and murmuring, 'I want you now. I need you inside me…'

She felt him reach down to open a door. His shoulders were rigid beneath her fingers, the muscles as hard as marble, and he strode quickly across a room, his footsteps echoing on bare boards. Sophie lifted her head and looked.

The room they had entered was huge, circular and empty except for a hulking great chest of drawers, a magnificent carved wooden bed. Kit set her down beside it. Evening light slanted through a mullioned window, washing the white walls pink. His eyes were black chasms of arousal as he slid his arms around her, reaching for the zip of her dress.

'This time,' he whispered throatily, 'we take it slowly. You're too beautiful to be rushed.'

Without taking his eyes off her, he pulled it down, millimetre by millimetre. Sophie let out a shuddering breath, every atom of her resisting the urge to tear it off and then rip the shirt from his back, yank his trousers open. He trailed his fingers down her bare back, beneath the open zip. His eyes burned and a muscle jumped above his clenched jaw. She could tell what it cost him, this holding back. Frowning, almost as if he were in pain, he took hold of her shoulders and turned her round.

Sophie shivered as he swept aside her hair with his fingers. Her fingers curled into fists as his lips brushed the nape of her neck. In the silence she could hear the cry of the gulls wheeling through the apricot sky outside, the kiss of Kit's lips against her skin.

His fingers slid the strap of her dress off one shoulder, then the other. It fell to the floor.

She turned round, trembling with the need to feel his skin on hers. He took a small, indrawn breath as he looked down at her body—naked except for a pair of lilac lace knickers—and with shaking fingers she began to undo the buttons of his shirt.

She wasn't sure she could match his self-control. She had to bite down on the insides of her cheeks to stop herself from ripping the remaining buttons from their holes. Looking up she saw that his face wore an expression of intense focus.

In contrast, his eyes were hooded, gleaming with want. She reached the last button, and they flickered closed for a second.

'Kit—'

He took a step backwards, sinking down onto the edge of the bed and keeping his eyes fixed on hers as he kissed her midriff. Her muscles contracted in a sharp spasm of want and she gripped his shoulders, anchoring herself against the delicious tension that was already beginning to build as his mouth moved lower and he eased her knickers down.

She let out a high, desperate whimper.

But he was relentless. With maddening slowness his fingers caressed her thighs while his tongue probed and explored. Her head fell back and she thrust her hips forwards, upwards, writhing and rotating as he breathed heat against her and his tongue found her clitoris.

Sophie fell forwards, burying her face in his hair. Feeling the violent shudders of her orgasm wrack her, he held her waist and pulled her back onto the bed with him. Kicking off his trousers, he was inside her in seconds, moaning as he felt her slippery wetness close around him.

For a moment they both stilled, their gazes locked. Then, very slowly, she reached up to kiss his lips.

'I love you.'

It was little more than a shivering breath, but it shattered his self-control. Gathering her into his arms, he cradled her against his chest, and she wrapped her legs tightly around his waist as he drove into her, strong thrusts that took him to the brink. Feeling her convulse around him again tipped him over the edge.

Ecstasy rocked him. In that moment it was possible to believe he was immortal.

'Kit?'

Sophie's head was resting on his chest, the beat of his heart keeping time with the distant rhythm of the waves below. She was dazed with happiness and the relief of being close to him again.

'Mmm?'

His voice rumbled like distant thunder deep in his chest. Love blossomed inside her and a smile spread across her face.

'I hate to ruin the poetry of the moment, but I'm absolutely starving.'

'That could be a problem,' he said gravely, tracing a lazy circle with a fingertip on her shoulder. 'I have no idea what time it is, but the shop in the village will have closed ages ago and I'm not sure there'll be anything in the kitchen. Do you want to drive to Hawksworth for dinner?'

Sophie considered for a moment as ripples of pleasure spread down her arm and through her whole body.

'Would it mean getting dressed?'

'Probably. They're quite old-fashioned about things like that round here.'

'In that case, let's not bother.' Rolling reluctantly away from him, Sophie swung her legs over the edge of the bed and stood up shakily. 'Jasper will just have to sacrifice his Toblerone. And we have champagne.'

'We have an entire cellar full of it, in fact,' Kit remarked dryly.

'Oh, yes. I suppose so. I didn't think of that.'

She bent down to pick up her dress, which was buried under his hastily discarded trousers. As she moved them something fell out of the pocket and skidded across the polished floor.

It was a box. A square, black velvet box.

Without thinking, Sophie went to pick it up. It was only when she was standing there, holding it in her hand and staring down at it, that her brain caught up and she realised what it might be.

Her jaw dropped. Hope and joy and excitement ballooned

inside her as she lifted her head to look at him. For a second she could only think of how incredibly sexy he looked, sprawled against the white sheets in the dying light. And then she noticed his face. It was frighteningly blank.

'Kit?' Her voice was a dried-up whisper. Her heart was beating very hard, as if the blood in her veins had turned to treacle. 'What's this?'

He sat up slowly, the muscles in his stomach and shoulders moving beneath the bronzed skin as he raised a hand and raked it through his hair in what looked like a gesture of resignation.

'Open it.'

Her hands were shaking, making it difficult to unhook the tiny catch. The lid of the box opened with a soft creak. Sophie gasped.

The ring had a polished stone of iridescent green at its centre, but her hand was shaking so much that it caught the rose-pink rays of sun and made a rainbow of other colours shimmer in its depths. It was circled by a double row of diamonds. There was no doubt that it was very old, and very, very valuable.

She also had the feeling she'd seen it before.

'It's a black opal,' he said tonelessly. 'It's called The Dark Star. It's been a family engagement ring for generations.'

A memory stirred in the back of her mind. 'Ah,' she said with an uneasy laugh. 'Is this that awkward moment when your girlfriend accidentally discovers the family ring you're saving to give to someone who has the right breeding to wear it?' Shutting the box again, she held it out to him. 'You'd better keep it somewhere safe.'

'Come here,' he drawled softly.

She went towards him on trembling legs. Gently he took the box from her and pulled out the ring. Taking hold of her left hand, he brushed his lips over the hennaed vine tendril that snaked down her third finger before sliding the ring onto it.

'Is that safe enough?'

He pulled her back down onto the bed, taking her face in his hands and kissing her so that she wouldn't see the despair and self-loathing in his eyes.

CHAPTER TEN

'THAT'LL be twenty-two pounds fifty-six please. I'll put it on the Fitzroy account, shall I, Miss...?'

Fumbling in her purse, Sophie looked up. From behind a forest of neon windmills and plastic beach spades on the counter Mrs Watts was looking at her with an air of beady expectation.

'Oh. It's G-Greenham,' she stuttered, caught off guard. 'Sophie Greenham. But no, thanks, I'll pay for it now.'

'But you're staying up at the castle, are you?' Mrs Watts persisted as she waited for the money, her killer interrogation skills masked by a veneer of friendliness and a polyester overall. 'With Master Kit? Or His Lordship as I'd still like to think of him. Such a shame. He's so much better suited to the role than Master Jasper—flighty, he is, always has been, a bit like his mother, the second Lady Fitzroy. In America now, so I gather.'

'Yes,' Sophie confirmed helplessly, handing over the money and glancing back towards the door in the hope that rescue was about to come in the form of a large party of noisy children in search of buckets and spades and bags of sweets for the beach.

It wasn't.

'Oh-h-h, now that's a beautiful ring,' Mrs Watts said avidly, taking the notes Sophie offered, her eyes gleaming like

those of a sparrowhawk that had just spotted a fat baby rab-
bit as they fixed on The Dark Star. Sophie had no alternative than to keep her left hand extended as Mrs Watts leaned
through the plastic windmills to examine it. Thank goodness
the henna tattoo had faded. 'I think it's nonsense what they
say about opals being unlucky, don't you? I remember seeing
this on the first Lady Fitzroy. Lady Juliet.' She beamed up at
Sophie. 'Congratulations are in order, then, Miss Greenham?'

'Sophie. Yes.'

Beaming, Mrs Watts placed a hand on her ample, polyes-
ter-encased bosom. 'Oh, I'm so thrilled. Master Kit is such
a gentleman, and it's a good many years since there was a
proper wedding at the castle.' She began gathering up Sophie's
purchases and putting them all into a carrier bag. 'Sir Ralph
got hitched to his second wife down in London—she never
did like it up here much—but I still remember the day he
and Lady Juliet got married. The whole village turned out to
watch her father walk her into church.' She paused, a bunch
of rust-coloured chrysanthemums clutched in her hand like
a bridal bouquet, a distant, dreamy look in her eyes. 'Oh, she
was a picture, she was…and a *proper* lady. She would never
have let the castle get into the state it has. Such a shame it
didn't last.'

Sophie resisted the urge to tell her not to expect a 'proper'
wedding at the castle any time soon. Taking advantage of Mrs
Watts's lapse into reminiscence, she grabbed the carrier bag
and moved towards the door.

'Here, you're forgetting your flowers. Lovely ones they
are too; Mr Watts's pride and joy—prize winners.' Mrs Watts
came round the counter to give them to her and then, bound
by some weird feudal imperative, hurried over to open the
door for her. Sophie felt herself blush with embarrassment.

'Thank you, but I can manage—'

'Nonsense,' Mrs Watts said stoutly. 'You've a position in
this village now. We're very proud of our heritage.'

Acutely conscious of her cheap chain-store dress and sneakers, Sophie went out into the late-summer sunshine. The school term had just started again so the village had emptied of holidaymakers, but there was a small group of young mothers with pushchairs standing chatting beside the green. Sophie felt a pang of longing so strong it took her breath away for a second. Her period, usually relentlessly regular, was three days late. Impulsively she turned back to Mrs Watts.

'What *do* they say about opals being unlucky?'

She flapped a dismissive hand. 'Oh, it's just a silly old wives' tale. I don't go in for any of that kind of thing at all—horoscopes and star signs and all that hocus pocus. It's love makes a marriage work. Love and trust and talking to each other. That's what's kept me and Mr Watts together for almost fifty years.'

Oh, dear, Sophie thought wistfully as she walked back up to the castle, it didn't look good for her and Kit, then. Talking wasn't exactly the area in which their relationship was strongest. The closeness they'd shared that night when he'd given her the ring had begun to fade again, almost from the moment he'd put it on her finger. During the days that followed Kit had been busy seeing solicitors, accountants, surveyors; picking his way through the legal tangle surrounding Leo's will and trying to organise the work that was needed immediately to keep the castle—long neglected by Ralph—standing.

In the evenings they ate, usually in front of the fire in the drawing room, or walked on the beach. They talked, of course, about the work that needed doing, but it was more about Alnburgh's future than their own. In fact, the most in-depth conversation she'd had about that was in a twenty-five-minute phone call with Jasper over a faint line to LA. As she'd predicted, the latest unforeseen development in the drama of Alnburgh's ownership had come as a huge relief to him, but his happiness was tempered with concern for her.

'It's hardly a cosy love nest to start married life in,' he'd sighed, with his usual ability to voice her own thoughts.

Her initial hope that their stay at Alnburgh might just be a brief one had faded as the days slipped past and Kit got more deeply involved in the business of the estate. Sophie could see how much he cared about it, and it was clear he had no plans to return to London. For his sake she would just have to try to get used to thinking of Alnburgh as home.

Her pace had got slower the nearer she got to the castle, and going from the buttery sunshine into the armoury hall was like stepping into a crypt. She walked quickly through the long gallery, steadfastly refusing to let herself look up at the animal heads to see if their eyes were following her as she went, and down the steps into the kitchen.

It was an enormous, gloomy room with a vaulted ceiling and a Victorian cast-iron range built into one end. The rest of it wasn't much more contemporary, and the only light came from rows of windows set high up in the stone walls, and a nineteen-thirties enamel lamp that hung over the enormous table. It was a far cry from the sunny, friendly kitchen she had half imagined when she'd told Jasper that she was ready for a home.

Sophie put the shopping onto the table and went in search of a vase for the flowers. She had discovered a whole room further along the corridor entirely devoted to china of all sorts—tureens, coffee pots, rose bowls and no doubt a large selection of vases too—but she didn't dare take anything from there in case it turned out to be too rare and valuable for Mr Watts's chrysanthemums. Instead she took a plain cream jug from the dresser and filled it with water.

In an attempt to bridge the gap between herself and Kit, she'd decided to cook properly tonight, and lay the table in the dining room for the first time since they'd been at Alnburgh. She'd spent what seemed to her to be a ridiculous amount of money on a fillet of venison from the tiny butcher's shop in the village, mainly because it sounded appropriately posh to be dished up in such formal surroundings.

She picked up the jug with the flowers in and carried it back upstairs to the dining room. It was pitch black, the tall windows hidden by shutters and heavy velvet curtains. The urge to go and throw them both open was almost overwhelming, but Sophie resisted. She had made that mistake on the first day as she'd gone around trying to lighten the oppressive gloom that filled the rooms, but Kit had told her that light was bad for the paintings, and that the Victorian curtains couldn't withstand being opened and closed too often.

Instead she flicked the light switch, and the gigantic chandelier over the table came on, along with the brass lights above the biggest portraits. Sophie put the jug of flowers on the table and stood back, hands on her hips, to look at it.

A great wave of misery and despair crashed over her.

It was hopeless, she realised. Mr Watts's chrysanthemums might be his pride and joy, but they certainly wouldn't win her any prizes for interior-design flair. Beside the other flowers standing in the buckets outside the village shop their mopheads had seemed huge, but here in the cavernous dining room they looked insignificant and lost.

Like her at Alnburgh.

All her efforts to make a difference, to put her mark on the place and make it feel like home, were utterly futile, she thought, blinking back tears. What was the use of lighting scented candles in the hall when nothing could ever shift the smell of cold stone, damp earth and age? What was the point of trying to make Alnburgh feel like hers when she was reminded of its previous occupants at every turn?

She lifted her head, looking at the painted faces that lined the walls. All of them seemed to look back at her with contempt in their hooded eyes. Except one.

It was the portrait Sophie had noticed on her first night at Alnburgh six months ago, and it showed a woman in a pink silk dress, with roses woven into her piled-up hair. What set her apart from the other sour-faced Fitzroys was her beauty and the secretive smile that played about her pink lips and gave her an air of suppressed mischief. Sophie remembered Ralph telling her that she was a music-hall singer who had caught the eye of the then earl, who had married her despite the fact that she was much younger and 'definitely not countess material'.

She shivered slightly as his voice came back to her. 'You and me both,' she muttered, and was about to turn away when something else caught her eye.

The girl's hands were folded in her lap, and on the left one, lovingly picked out by the artist's brush, was Sophie's ring.

So that was where she'd seen it before. A chill crept down her neck, as if it were being caressed by cold fingers. Lifting her hand, she looked from the real opal glinting dully in the twenty-first-century electric light, to the painted one on the finger of the eighteenth-century countess, remembering as she did so how her story had ended. Pregnant with a supposedly illegitimate child, suffering from advanced syphilis, the girl in the painting had thrown herself off the battlements in the east tower, to her death on the rocks below.

She hadn't known what Mrs Watts had meant about opals being unlucky, but she was beginning to get the picture. She knew of two Fitzroy brides who'd worn the ring before her, and neither had lasted long at Alnburgh.

Rainbow had been a great believer in signs and portents; messages in everything from tea leaves to constellations. Growing up, Sophie had always dismissed it as yet another of her mother's many eccentricities.

Hurrying quickly from the dining room, switching off the light, she suddenly wasn't so sure.

'The trust was set up some twenty-eight years ago now, with myself as one of the trustees. The others were the then Lady

Fitzroy, an army colleague of Leo's, the senior partner in the firm of accountants he used…'

Kit's attention began to wander. He had been on the phone to various people all day—all week, it seemed—and his head and neck and brain ached with the effort of trying to make sense of Alnburgh's financial and legal position. It was nightmarishly complicated and excruciatingly dull, however it did give him something to think about besides Sophie, and the fact that he'd pretty much ruined her life.

As Leo's elderly former solicitor went on Kit noticed that the library had darkened and filled with shadows. He felt a flicker of surprise. The room's huge oriel window looked out over the beach below, and through it Kit could see that the mood of the sea had changed and that huge, swollen purple clouds had gathered over the headland to the south.

'We took a great deal of trouble over the wording of the document to ensure there were no loopholes for Ralph Fitzroy's legal team to use to his advantage…'

A week ago the beach had been scattered with groups of people—families with buckets and spades enjoying the last few days of their holidays, teenagers from the village with a radio and illicit bottles of cider—but now it was pretty much empty. A dog galloped along the wet sand, ears flapping, and in the distance a slim figure stood at the edge of the sea, her green cotton dress blowing up in the sudden brisk wind, her red hair flying.

A lightning fork of desire snapped through him, closely followed by a crash of guilt and despair. God, he loved her. But seeing her out there, standing in front of the swelling sea, only seemed to emphasise that elusive, untamable quality she had that had drawn him to her from the start.

And which made putting that bloody ring on her finger even more unforgivable.

That had been his chance to tell her, but he had let it pass because he knew that it would set in motion a chain of events that was entirely out of his control. She would want him to see a doctor. And then, if the doctor's diagnosis confirmed his fears, he would have to let her go.

And he wasn't ready to do that yet. He'd only just found her. He wanted to make this happiness last for as long as he could.

He lifted the hand that wasn't holding the phone and looked at it. The pins-and-needles sensation hadn't been as bad since they'd returned to Alnburgh, and there were times when it disappeared altogether. Most notably when he was in bed with Sophie, touching her body, feeling her satin skin against his fingertips. Then he could believe that it wasn't as serious as he thought...

'Lord Fitzroy? Are you still there?'

'Yes. Sorry.' Kit dragged his attention back to the voice on the other end of the phone. 'Perhaps you could repeat that?'

'I said, the fact that the trust was set up so long before Leo Fitzroy's death means that the amount of inheritance tax owing is substantially reduced.'

'That's excellent news,' Kit said blandly. In fact, it was the news he'd been holding out for, and the key to securing Alnburgh's future, but at that moment it was slightly over-shadowed by a sudden raging need to drag Sophie back here and take her upstairs.

'It was partly chance, of course. When the trust was set up we didn't know how long Mr Fitzroy would live, and frankly didn't expect it to be more than the statutory seven-year period that would put Alnburgh out of danger from death duties. It was just lucky that he survived much longer than that.'

That was a matter of opinion, thought Kit, remembering the photographs Juliet had shown him chronicling Leo's decline.

'Thanks,' he said brusquely, impatient to end the call. Outside the sky had darkened menacingly and the seagulls were being thrown off course by the wind. Sophie didn't have a coat. She was going to get soaked.

Bringing the conversation to a swift close, he put down the phone and strode to the door. He went down the back stairs, kicking off his shoes and grabbing one of the many water-proofs that hung in the boot room before going out through the east-gate door. From this side of the castle a steep path cut through the dune grass down to the beach. Dark purple clouds moved in from the south like an invading army and the first drops of rain were already falling.

He began to run. Up ahead, in the distance he could see that Sophie had turned and was beginning to make her way back. She broke into a run but at that moment the clouds un-leashed the full force of their fury.

It felt like standing beneath a hail of bullets. In a matter of seconds Kit was drenched, as was the waterproof he carried. Not that it would do much good now anyway, but he ran on, his feet pounding against the hard sand. As they got closer to each other he heard Sophie's whoop of exhilaration and saw that she was laughing.

His weary heart soared. Suddenly nothing mattered—not the whole legal mess or Alnburgh or the money or anything. Not even the future. Nothing existed beyond that moment on the empty, rain-lashed beach, the water running down his face and sticking his clothes to his skin, the woman he loved running towards him, laughing.

'It's *insane*!' she cried, throwing her arms out wide and turning round, tipping her face up to the deluge.

Barely breaking his stride, he caught hold of her waist and scooped her up into his arms. The wind took her shriek of joy, tossing it up to the angry sky. Her body was warm and pliant, her heart beating hard against his ribs.

'We might as well give in to it and just get wet,' she gasped. 'It's miles back to the castle—even *you* can't possibly run all the way back carrying me.'

'I'm not even going to try.'

He had turned his back on the sea and was heading up the beach, his pace slowing as he reached the softer, deeper sand at the top. The rain fell more heavily than ever. It ran down his face, blurring his vision. He shook his head to clear the water from his eyes so that he could see the narrow path through the marram grass, leading up over the dunes.

'Where are we going?'

'You'll see.'

It was steeper than he remembered and the sand slipped away beneath his feet, but the need to get out of the rain and peel the wet clothes from Sophie's delicious body gave him superhuman strength. In seconds they had crested the dune.

The farmhouse was right in front of them, just as he'd remembered it.

'Oh, what a gorgeous house!' She almost had to shout to be heard above the noise of the downpour. 'Do you know the people who own it?'

'Yes.'

Pushing open the little wooden gate, he strode up the path, hoisting Sophie harder against him while he freed a hand to key in the code. He sent up a wry prayer of thanks for the lack of imagination and security-consciousness that had made Ralph choose Tatiana's birth-date as the access code for the entire estate.

'You can put me down, you know…' Sophie murmured, catching a raindrop that was running down his cheek with her tongue.

'Uh-uh. Not yet. I'm not letting you go.'

The door swung open and he carried her over the threshold, his heart twisting as he was hit by the symbolism of the gesture. Kicking the door shut behind them, abruptly silencing the noise of the rain, he gently set Sophie down.

She turned, leaning her back against him as she looked around the large, low-beamed farmhouse kitchen.

'I feel like Goldilocks,' she said wonderingly, taking his hand and pulling him across to the table so she could peer into the basket that had been left there. 'So who does own this?'

Kit could feel the warmth of her skin through their wet clothes, the rounded firmness of her bottom. His voice was gruff with suppressed desire as he replied.

'The estate.'

She picked up a bottle of wine from the basket, a packet of biscuits. 'So that means you, Lord Fitzroy.' She turned to kiss him lightly on the mouth. 'Can I look around?'

'Be my guest.'

Still with her fingers laced through his, she led him out of the kitchen, their sandy feet making no sound on the stone flags. Beyond it there was a square hallway with a stately old staircase going up, doors leading through to other rooms. Sophie opened one, and breathed in the scent of woodsmoke as she looked into a long room with a fireplace. A huge bay window that flooded the room with rain-soaked light and looked out onto the beach.

There was an odd feeling in her chest as they went quickly on, through rooms that felt as if they were holding their breaths. Waiting for her. Upstairs she opened the door into a child's room, with a little bed covered by a blue quilt with ducks on it, and a cot. Through the streaming rain on the window she could see a swing in the garden below.

Her whole body throbbed with yearning. Stricken, she turned to Kit, opening her mouth to say something, but the words stuck in her swollen throat.

Gently he pulled her back towards the door.

'I'm afraid I'm going to have to move the tour on at this point,' he said huskily, brushing the side of her neck with his lips in the way that always made her instantly boneless with need. 'Allow me to show you the master bedroom...'

When she broke away from kissing him and opened her

eyes again Sophie found herself in a large, low room with a pretty fireplace and a window like the one in the sitting room downstairs. A window seat was set into it.

As she looked Kit was very slowly turning her round so he could undo the zip on her dripping dress. Rain rattled against the window, and longing beat within her with the same relentless insistence. For him; but not just for the quick, exhilarating release of making love.

For more.

For all of him—body and soul. Head and heart. For always.

Her dress fell to the floor. She stood before him, naked and trembling, and for the first time ever she didn't reach to tear his clothes off, rushing and fumbling.

They gazed at each other for a long moment. His silver eyes were hooded. The bruising on his face was gone now, the cuts healed, though the small scars they left would always be there. Mutely she reached up to run her fingers over them. He caught her hand, pressing it to his cheek for a second, then drawing her gently over to the bed. In one deft movement he folded down the covers, then picked her up and laid her onto the cool sheets.

She lay still as he peeled off his T-shirt and reached for the buckle of his belt. Her need for him was as strong as ever—stronger if anything—but it was as if something had shifted inside her; something to do with the quiet bedroom with the uneven walls and slightly sloping floor in this old farmhouse. It was as if she had been running for a long time, hurrying to get somewhere, and at last she had arrived. There was no need to rush any more.

His naked body was so beautiful. Her breath hitched in her throat as he lowered himself onto the bed beside her and, pulling the covers over them both, folded her gently into his arms.

After the rain the sky was washed out and new. The sun reappeared, making the raindrops on the window sparkle like crystals. Like the tears on Sophie's lashes. The intensity of their lovemaking had shaken them both.

'I *like* this house,' she said softly now, breaking the silence that had wrapped itself around them since the sobbing cries of her orgasm had faded.

'Do you come here a lot?'

'I used to call in a lot when I was a kid,' he said gravely. 'But I have to say that this is the first time I've actually come here.'

He'd said it in an attempt to lighten the atmosphere a little and banish the mood of wistfulness that seemed to have stolen the laughter from Sophie's lips and the sparkle from her eyes as they'd looked round the house. It worked. She gave one of her breathy giggles. 'Don't be silly. You know what I mean.'

Smiling, he kissed the top of her head. 'OK. I used to walk down here when I was home from school for the holidays, after Jasper was born. It was a working farm then; the people who lived here were called Mr and Mrs Prior. They were good to me. Probably because they felt sorry for me— it must have been obvious to everyone that I was surplus to requirement after Ralph remarried and Jasper arrived. They let me help out on the farm when I was old enough.'

He'd often eaten with them too; food he could still remember, that was nothing like the bland boarding-school stodge or the fussy, formal meals served up in the Alnburgh dining room, accompanied by acerbic asides from Ralph. It was here that he'd learned for the first time what 'home' could mean, and understood why some boys cried in the dark for the first few nights of term.

'They sound lovely,' Sophie said. 'What happened to them?'

'They went the same way as all the other tenants when Tatiana decided she'd like a little project and turned all the estate cottages into holiday lets. It wasn't too bad for them—

they were looking to retire anyway—but a lot of local people lost homes their families had lived in for generations. The idea was she was going to be completely in charge of managing them all, but of course the moment the fun decorating bit was done she got bored and handed it all over to an agency.'

'Ah.' It was a soft sigh of disappointment. 'So it's still being let? I was hoping we could stay.' She sat up suddenly, clutching the duvet against her breasts. 'Wait a minute—the basket on the table—does that mean people are going to be arriving today? Now I really do feel like Goldilocks—any minute someone's going to appear and shout, "Who's been shagging in my bed?"'

Kit smiled. He couldn't help it.

'Changeover day is usually Friday, so we should be safe. We can use the stuff the agency have left and I'll replace it tomorrow. Shall we open the wine?'

It was almost a rhetorical question, since Sophie had never been known to refuse wine before, but she hesitated for a second, then sank down beside him again, not meeting his eye.

'No, but I'd kill for a cup of tea. How much does it cost to stay here? I'm seriously thinking of booking it for as long as I can afford.'

CHAPTER ELEVEN

Sophie slipped down beneath the warm fragrant water and, sighing, closed her eyes.

She was having a bath in Tatiana's bathroom because it was by far the most comfortable one at Alnburgh, having been updated by her interior designer with no regard for expense. Or, unfortunately, for taste. Even behind her closed lids Sophie was still dazzled by the glare of about a hundred spotlights glinting off polished marble, gold-plated taps and wall-to-wall mirrors.

Alnburgh was all about extremes. Half of it hadn't been touched in a hundred years, and the other half had been tarted up to look like Selfridges' window at Christmastime. Neither half was particularly attractive or comfortable to live in. Wistfully Sophie let her mind drift back to that afternoon at the farmhouse.

When Kit was downstairs making the tea she had got up and stripped the bed, then set about clumsily remaking it with fresh sheets she'd found in the linen cupboard. She could hear him moving about in the kitchen below, and the sense of his presence near her in the house, the simple domesticity of the task, had given her an absurd sense of satisfaction.

The skies had cleared and the beach had been bathed in golden sunlight as they'd walked back, but the castle had loomed blackly ahead of them, looking so like a picture of a haunted house in a cartoon that Sophie had almost expected to see a flash of forked lightning above the battlements and hear the sound of evil laughter.

Even the sand beneath her feet had felt cold in the shadow of Alnburgh, and with every step she had almost been able to feel Kit slipping away from her again. She had a sudden vision of the castle as a rival—the Other Woman, so much more sophisticated and enthralling than her. Or maybe she was the impostor? The mistress who would never quite win Kit back from his demanding, capricious wife.

She hauled herself up out of the water and reached for a towel. She wanted to be his wife, she thought sadly. She wanted normality, a kitchen that wasn't in a dungeon, a swing in the garden and a cot in the bedroom upstairs. And a baby... Oh, please, God, *a baby...*

The Dark Star glinted in the spotlights as she wrapped the towel around herself and stepped out of the bath, and out of the warm water she was aware of a dragging pain in her stomach. Reaching down to dry herself, she felt a thud of foreboding and looked down at the damp red stain on the pale blue bath towel.

A sob rose in her throat.

There was no baby.

'That's great news, Randall.'

Kit slumped against the desk in the library, squeezing his eyes shut as he processed the latest information on Lewis's progress and fighting against the now-familiar onslaught of guilt and relief.

'Isn't it?' From the other end of the phone, in the Birmingham hospital, Randall sounded so positive it was almost infectious. 'Of course the fact that Lewis is a young, fit guy has definitely been on his side in helping him recover physically, and this baby arriving in the next few weeks has given him a real goal to work towards in terms of getting out of hospital. Hopefully he should make it in time for the birth.'

'How's his family coping?' Standing up, Kit went to the window. The view was entirely different from the one he'd seen earlier; the distant sea was quiet and the expanse of sand was wide and flat and clean now the storm had passed.

'His family are rallying round, and so are their entire neighbourhood and all his mates, planning a big party for when he gets home.' Randall paused before adding tersely, 'The girlfriend is less of a support. I wouldn't put money on her sticking with him long term. I just hope she has the decency to stay with him until he's back on his feet again, however long it takes.'

Kit kept his voice deliberately neutral and his eyes fixed on the distant place where the sea met the sky. 'I don't suppose it's easy for her either, you know. She's just a kid too. She didn't exactly sign up for any of this when she started going out with him.'

'Maybe you're right.' Randall sighed. 'Sorry. It's been a long shift and I've lost perspective a bit. Anyway, how are you?'

As he spoke movement out of the corner of Kit's eye made him turn his head. His heart crashed as icy sweat drenched his body and his palms burned. A man with a metal detector was making his way slowly over the sand and for a moment Kit was back in uniform, watching his team mates inch up a dusty road, looking for mines.

'Kit?'

Randall's voice made the nightmarish vision fade again. Kit squeezed his eyes tightly shut for a second. 'Sorry. I'm fine.' His left hand hung at his side and he stretched and squeezed his numb fingers. 'Tell Lewis I'll come and see him tomorrow.'

'I'm here if you need me, remember,' Randall prompted gently.

'I'll bear it in mind. Thanks.'

His hand was shaking as he hung up.

He didn't want to know, he told himself angrily. There was no need.

Quickly he crossed the room and headed for the stairs to find Sophie. Suddenly he had the terrible, crushing insight that every hour, every second with her was precious because there might only be a finite number of them...

The bedroom door was shut. He stopped outside it, leaning his head against it for a moment, breathing hard, reining back his thoughts before they raced away, completely out of control. God. And he'd always been so rigidly in command— of himself and everything else. So rational. So unemotional.

He barely recognised that man any more. The good soldier. The strong leader. The man who cared about little and had even less to lose.

Now he cared so much it was killing him. And he had everything to lose.

Gently he knocked and pushed open the door. Wrapped in a light blue bath towel, Sophie was sitting at the little oak console table she had brought up to use as a dressing table, brushing her hair. The pink-tinged evening light made her bare skin look as soft and tempting as a marshmallow. Kit's stomach muscles tightened as if against a punch.

He went to stand behind her. She didn't stop brushing, or raise her eyes to meet his in the mirror. Its age-mottled glass gave her face a timeless, ethereal beauty that seemed to place her somewhere just beyond his reach. He needed to reassure himself that she was there, that she was his, and he lifted his hand to sweep the heavy fall of her hair sideways and bent to kiss the nape of her neck.

She was the only thing that anchored him to sanity, the only way he knew of keeping the demons at bay. He breathed in her scent, and was aware of the fizzing in his fingers subsiding as they met her warm flesh.

'Did you ring the hospital?' she said in a low voice, bowing her head forwards as he kissed her neck.

'Um-hm.' Preoccupied, Kit didn't lift his head.

'How's Lewis?'

'Better.'

She leaned forwards, stiffening a little and moving away from him. 'What does that mean? Better as in "completely recovered and going home"? Or better as in "off the critical list"?'

He didn't want to think about it. Her skin was like velvet against his lips, and he put his arms around her to peel away the towel.

'Somewhere between the two.'

Her hands came up to cover his and his first thought was that, as so often, she had read his mind, but then he felt her getting to her feet and pushing his hands away.

'Kit, stop.'

Instantly he jerked upright and took a step back. Pulling the towel more tightly around herself, Sophie sank down onto the little rosewood chair again, her head lowered so that he couldn't see her face.

'What's wrong?'

She gave a slight shrug, but didn't look up. 'You tell me.'

He sighed, dragging a hand impatiently over his eyes, a feeling of unease prickling at the back of his neck. 'Sorry, I don't get it. Is this going to be one of those cryptic conversations in which I have to guess what's going on in your head?'

'Maybe. At least then you'd know what it's like for me.'

Her voice was low, but the edge of bitterness in it was unmistakable. Unease turned to alarm, making him speak more coldly than he'd intended.

'What's that supposed to mean?'

'It means I can't go on letting you push me away and shut me out.'

Kit gave a harsh bark of laughter. 'Forgive me for being pedantic, but weren't you the one who just pushed me away?'

'That's *sex*, Kit! I'm talking about intimacy. *Talking.*' Her voice trembled with emotion, and as she raised her head he saw her face properly.

'You've been crying. Sophie, what's wrong?'

Shock hit him hard, like a punch to the solar plexus. She never cried—except when she saw a spider, or in the aftermath of their lovemaking when she collapsed, gasping and sobbing, onto his chest. Bewildered, he paced across the floor, his mind going back over the afternoon as he tried to think what could possibly have brought this on.

'Look, if you hate it here that much…'

She shook her head, quickly rubbing the tears away with the back of her hand. 'It's not that. Not really. I mean, it's not what I would have chosen, but I'd happily live in a cave as long as I was with you.'

'You *are* with me.'

'No. I'm not.' She looked up again, and her eyes met his in the mirror. They shimmered with tears and were filled with an aching sadness. 'We sleep together, Kit. We have sex—a lot of sex. Sometimes we have breakfast together the morning after, but we don't talk. Not about anything that matters.'

'Like what?'

'Like about the future.' She took a quick breath, in and out. 'Or the past for that matter. Like what the hell happened to you while you were away.'

'There's nothing to talk about.' Gritting his teeth, he spoke with exaggerated patience. 'Things happen all the time out there. Bloody awful things that would drive you crazy if you let yourself dwell on them. But you don't. You leave them there and you come home and forget.'

'OK. I get it. You don't want to talk to me.' She gave a crooked smile that was unbearably poignant. 'But I need to talk to you. Five months is a long time and stuff happened here that I haven't had a chance to tell you about.'

'What stuff?' His blood ran to ice.

'Nothing terrible. But we do need to discuss it. I did as you said and went to see a doctor. About my periods.'

'And?'

'It's endometriosis.' She looked down at the hairbrush in her hand, turning it over and over. 'No surprises there, but he warned me that getting pregnant might be difficult. He told me not to leave it too long before trying to start a family and—'

'Sophie—'

She ignored the warning in his tone, looking straight at him with a mixture of resignation and defiance. 'I stopped taking the pill immediately.'

Kit spun away from her. It was as if a switch had been flicked inside his body, shutting off all function, all feeling for a few seconds, while his brain spun into freefall. *Ten per cent of cases.* He raised his hands to his head as the implications hit.

'And that was before I got home?' he rasped. 'So for the last *two weeks* we've—'

'I'm not pregnant.'

The bald, emotionless statement stilled the panic in his head.

He dropped his hands to his sides again. Acid fizzed beneath his skin, burning and throbbing in the pulse points on his wrists just as horror beat inside him at the realisation that keeping his fears to himself could have had such far-reaching consequences. But more immediate than that was relief.

'I'm sorry,' he said, turning to face her, but his voice was hoarse and unconvincing even to his ears.

'Are you?' Sophie stood up, stepping out from behind the dressing table chair and turning to him with eyes that blazed with fury. 'Because for a moment there I could have sworn

that sorry was the last thing you were. In fact, "hugely re-lieved" might be a better way of describing your reaction.' She held up her hands as if to push him back. 'I wouldn't bother to deny it, Kit. There's really no point. I'm not even surprised, since it's been getting increasingly obvious that there's no fu-ture for us. Tell me, were you waiting out of kindness to let me down gently, or were you just going to shut me out a bit more every day in the hope that eventually I'd go of my own accord, and leave you free to mingle your exclusive Fitzroy genes with someone of the right pedigree?'

Every barbed word tore into him, but he knew he had brought the pain on himself. He gritted his teeth and steeled himself for more.

'No.'

Tossing her hair back, she laughed, but it came out more like a sob. It hurt him even more than her anger and her in-accurate accusations. 'Oh, dear. You'll have to do better than that, Kit,' she said. 'This is the part where you're supposed to take me in your arms and tell me I've got it all wrong and promise that one day we'll have a family of our own—or didn't you read the script?'

It took all his strength, all his courage to meet her eyes. He felt as if he'd swallowed arsenic.

'I can't do that. I'm sorry.'

Darkness gathered behind Sophie's eyes. Her head was filled with a strange buzzing sound, and for a moment she actu-ally thought she was going to faint. Kit's face swam in front of her, as hard and blank as if it had been carved from stone.

'There's something I have to tell you.'

His emotionless voice reached her from a long distance away. He turned away from her then, and she was grateful that he couldn't see her grabbing hold of the chest of draw-ers for support as she fought to drag in a breath. Her stomach cramped.

It was hardly a bolt from the blue. She had seen it coming since the morning after their dinner at Villa Luana. She had to hold onto her dignity.

'It's OK,' she said in a strangled voice. 'You don't have to explain. I understand already. When you asked me to marry you, all this wasn't part of the deal.' She made a gesture with her hand that inadequately indicated the vast castle that stretched all around them. 'I know things have changed since then.'

'Yes. Things have changed.' Kit sounded so infinitely weary that for a moment she almost felt sorry for him. 'But it's nothing to do with Alnburgh. It's me. I've changed.'

'Oh, God.' She actually managed a genuine laugh then, albeit a slightly hysterical one. '"It's not you, it's me." That's such an old line, Kit.'

He didn't smile. Standing in front of the window with another spectacular Alnburgh sunset spreading its glories across the sky behind him, he looked as stern and beautiful as a painted saint in the Sistine Chapel.

'It's true. I wish it wasn't but it is. I'm not the person—the hero...' his mouth twisted bleakly '...you think I am.'

Sophie was distantly aware that she was shivering. She should put some clothes on, but she couldn't quite bring herself to do it in front of him now. He was suddenly a stranger to her.

'You remember the incident that happened out there on the day I came back...' Kit bowed his head briefly '...the one that left a nineteen-year-old boy in Intensive Care with bullets in his head and back? I should have been looking after him, just like you said, but what happened to him was my fault. All. My. Fault.'

His voice dripped ice down her spine. He was standing against the window, his face in shadow, but his eyes burned with a peculiar intensity that made her breath catch and her heart ache with compassion and fear.

'That can't be true. Surely in an explosion—'

'He wasn't hurt in the explosion,' he said with exaggerated patience that sounded almost like scorn. 'He was hurt *before* the bomb went off, by enemy fire.'

'How can that be your fault?'

'Because he was one of the infantry team covering my back while I defused the device,' he said in a low, mocking voice. Turning round, he gripped the window sill and looked out over the beach, though Sophie had a feeling he wasn't seeing the tranquil sweep of Northumberland sand at all. 'We'd been called to a bridge over one of the main routes into a town notorious for its insurgent activity. The bomb was underneath it, but the whole situation was a nightmare. The site was visible for miles around, from hundreds of rooftops and windows and balconies. We can clear the area immediately around the device on the ground, but it's impossible to make a site like that safe. The only thing to do is to go in there and do the job quickly.'

Sophie was transfixed, standing shivering in the middle of the room, her arms wrapped around herself because she couldn't wrap them around him. Everything about him told her to keep away, from his white-knuckled grip on the window sill to the bunched muscles across his shoulders.

'I couldn't do it,' he said bitterly. 'I couldn't do it because I couldn't feel my fingers properly. My hands were shaking. I dropped the wire cutters, and all I could think about was you.' He paused, letting his head drop for a moment and exhaling a ragged breath. 'That was when the shooting started and I knew we were screwed. There was nothing to do but get out fast. I was running back to the vehicle when the bomb went off, but Lewis had already been hit.'

'Oh, Kit…' Like a sleepwalker, Sophie moved towards him, unable to stop herself from reaching out and touching him. 'It wasn't your fault—you have to believe that. It was an impossible situation. It could have happened to anyone.'

Slowly, levering himself away from the window sill, he turned to face her. His mouth was curved into a bleak parody of a smile that made her insides freeze.

'I don't think so.'

'What do you mean?'

'Everything made sense when my mother mentioned Leo's illness.' The smile twisted. 'You thought it was bad enough that I inherited Alnburgh from him, but I'm afraid it looks like that might be the least of my problems. At least I could walk away from Alnburgh.'

'You think you have the same thing he had?'

Sophie's voice was a cracked whisper. By contrast his was cold, flat, utterly matter-of-fact.

'I checked with a friend who's a doctor. The early signs are clumsiness and loss of sensation in the hands. According to Juliet, there's a hereditary factor in ten per cent of cases. And that's why I'm glad you're not pregnant.'

Instinctively Sophie went towards him, wanting only to take him in her arms. A cautious hope was beginning to steal through her combined with relief that at last she understood. He had finally opened up to her, and now she knew what the problem was it was a case of dealing with it, one thing at a time.

'You have to see someone,' she said gently, wrapping her arms around him. 'Find out for sure.'

'Do I?'

She wasn't sure which was worse, his laconic drawl or his rigid, unyielding body. She drew sharply away from him.

'Of course—the sooner we know the better, and then what-ever the facts are we can deal with them.' She swallowed hard, her heart pounding, an icy avalanche of dread smashing away the hope and relief. '*Together*. Whatever it is, we'll—'

He shook his head. 'No.'

Sophie's hand flew to her mouth, stopping the sob that

swelled in her throat. Kit sighed, looking at her with an unflinching, silvery gaze.

'If I have what my f-father had…' his eyelids flickered as he stumbled over the word 'father', but his tone was colder, harder than ever as he continued '…I won't sentence you to that slow death with me. I'd have to let you go.'

'No,' she said, shaking her head in disbelief. 'You can't mean that. You wouldn't throw away what we have because—'

'Yes.' His voice held a terrifying note of finality. 'I spoke to Juliet. I know what it would mean. If I have this illness, there's no way I can marry you, Sophie. I'm sorry.'

Sophie stepped backwards, fighting for air. She felt dizzy and disorientated, as if she'd just stepped off some kind of extreme fairground ride.

'I hope *so much* that you don't,' she said in an odd, breathless voice. 'No one deserves to go through that. But if that's how you feel…even if you don't have it, it's over for us anyway.'

Nausea rolled over her and for a moment she thought she might pass out, but, gripping the edge of the dressing table, she carried on.

'Marriage is supposed to be for better or for worse, in sickness and in health. It's supposed to be about facing things together. About trust and sharing and letting each other in, so maybe…'

She faltered again, staring at him across the space that separated them, willing him to cross it and take her in his arms and tell her she was right and he hadn't been thinking straight. But he didn't move. Didn't open his mouth to argue or stop her from saying the words she didn't want to speak.

'Maybe we never stood a chance.'

Her voice had dried up to a cracked whisper. He closed his eyes briefly, as if he was in pain.

'If that's what you think…I won't try to change your mind.'

For a moment they just gazed at each other. And then he turned and pulled the door open. His back was rigid with tension as he walked out, as if he was only holding himself in check with the greatest effort.

Sinking down onto the bed, Sophie listened to his footsteps recede as he went down the stairs. From outside the cries of the gulls sounded like maniacal laughter.

CHAPTER TWELVE

KIT didn't come to bed that night.

Sophie measured the long hours by the distant chiming of the clock in the clock tower and the gradual lightening of the sky. For the first time in her life, sleep eluded her and she understood what it was like for Kit to suffer the torment of insomnia.

That, however, was about as far as her understanding of Kit went.

In a few short hours the man she loved, the man whose body she knew intimately, inch by inch, had become a stranger to her. Although maybe that wasn't quite true, she thought, staring into the ashy light of dawn. Maybe he'd always been a stranger and she'd been fooled into thinking they were close because they had such breathtaking sex. She sat up, her heart racing sickeningly, drenched in sweat as she had a flashback to the hammam in the hotel, when she'd actually convinced herself that the bond they shared went beyond words.

How spectacularly naive that seemed now.

She dropped her head into her hands. She'd looked on getting married like the start of some big adventure. It hadn't mattered that she knew little about the place she was going to, she'd been looking forward to exploring; to the excitement of the journey, the challenges, the quiet moments of joy.

Now she felt as if she'd arrived to find everywhere locked and barred, and marked 'Private. Keep Out.' There was nothing to do but give up and go home.

Move on. Just like you always do, sneered a malicious little voice inside her head.

Throwing back the twisted covers, she stumbled out of bed, tensing against the fist of pain that tightened in her stomach. She loved him. Too much to just walk away, especially when there was a possibility he could be facing the hardest challenge of his life.

Outside a pale band of gold on the horizon heralded the new day. Sophie hoped it was a good omen. Clumsily she pulled on jeans beneath the shirt she'd slept in and headed for the door. She felt spacey with lack of sleep, although already the hours of restless darkness and the awful events that had preceded them had taken on a kind of nightmarish quality that she was suddenly desperate to banish.

Going along the corridor towards the main staircase, she broke into a half-run. Everything would look different this morning. Now it was all out in the open they just needed to talk it over properly. She wondered where he'd slept last night—if he'd slept at all. The library was as good a place as any to start looking for him...

But in the end she didn't get that far. As she reached the bottom of the stairs she heard the sound of footsteps in the long gallery and the metallic jingle of car keys. Crossing the portrait hall, she saw him through the archway. He was dressed—properly dressed, unlike her—and carrying his jacket as he headed towards the armoury hall.

'Kit?' She went towards him, fear beating through her.

He stopped and was perfectly still for a moment, as if he was steeling himself before turning to face her. When he did his expression was carefully blank.

'I didn't want to wake you.' He held up a pen and a piece

of Alnburgh-headed notepaper he must have brought through from the library. 'I was going to leave a note.'

Sophie's teeth were chattering, making it hard to speak. 'Saying what?'

'I'm going to see Lewis.' He tossed the paper and pen down on the side table. 'It's a four-hour drive so I need to get an early start if I'm going to get back tonight.'

'You're coming back?'

'Of course,' he said wearily, going towards the door. 'What else would I do?'

'I don't know. I thought…' Relief made her shaky and in-articulate as she followed him. 'I'm sorry about last night. I couldn't sleep thinking about it and how mad it is to let this come between us. You must have been through hell these last couple of weeks, worrying about it, and I'm so sorry that you went through that alone.' He slid back the bolts on the door and Sophie blinked as light flooded the gloomy hall, bring-ing with it a draft of cool autumn air. 'But you're not alone any more. Whatever happens now, we're in it together.'

Kit paused in the doorway. The clear morning light showed up the shadows of exhaustion beneath his eyes and reminded her with sudden poignancy of when he'd first come home, making her wish she could turn the clock back. He sighed, bowing his head.

'No, Sophie,' he said with quiet resignation. 'I meant what I said last night. I won't do it to you. You're the most amaz-ing, vibrant person I've ever met.' He reached out and brushed her cheek with his fingertips. 'I won't condemn you to a life of watching me die by degrees. It would be like burying you alive.'

Sophie gave a sharp, indrawn breath, as if she'd just had cold water thrown in her face. 'But I love you,' she gasped. 'Whatever happens, *I love you*…'

He went down the steps into the misty morning and, open-ing the car door, threw his jacket onto the passenger seat. 'You say that now—hell, I'm sure you even think you mean it, but for how long, Sophie?' Slamming the door, he swung round to face her again. 'If this is what I think it is, it'll change *everything* between us.'

'Except how I feel about you.'

'You can't say that for sure.'

The stone flags were icy beneath Sophie's bare feet as she walked over to the car, but it was nothing compared to the chill inside her. 'I can, but this isn't about me really, is it? This is about you. You can't get your head round it because you don't feel that way in return. Or—' She came to an abrupt halt as another thought occurred to her. 'Is it more than that? Is this about your inability to get past the fact that your mother walked out on you all those years ago?' She saw his eyes narrow, his body tense and gave a slightly wild laugh as she realised she'd hit a nerve. 'You're punishing me for what she did, and for Ralph, who stopped loving you as soon as he found out you weren't his son—'

'Enough.'

The word was torn from some primitive part of him. He whirled round and Sophie got a fleeting glimpse of the hard, bunched muscles in his arm as he swung his fist. She gave a high, terrified cry, instinctively ducking away from him and putting her hands up to shield her face. There was a sickening crack as his hand smashed down on the wing of the car with such force that the shiny black metal buckled.

And then silence.

Perhaps it was the pain that brought Kit back to his senses, perhaps it was hearing Sophie cry out like that, but the violent impulse passed as quickly as it had gripped him. For a moment he stayed completely still, his arms braced against the bonnet of the car, his head bent. The sound of his laboured breathing seemed to fill the gentle autumn morning.

Then, mustering all his strength, he straightened up and turned to Sophie.

She had shrunk back against the castle wall and was pressed against it, her arms wrapped tightly around herself as if in an attempt to contain the violent shudders that convulsed her. But it was her face that shocked him most. It wore the expression he had seen before on people who had witnessed terrible trauma. A waxy-pale mask of abject terror.

Remorse and self-disgust exploded inside his head, rocking him to the core. 'God, Sophie—I'm sorry, I—' Instinctively he moved towards her, thinking only of pulling her into his arms and comforting her, but as he reached out she flinched violently away.

'Please—no,' she said in a strangled voice he didn't recognise. Shrinking back from him, she closed her eyes, as if she were wishing him away. 'Just go. Now.'

For a moment he couldn't move. But then, because he knew he had forfeited every moral and personal right when he'd lost control, he walked round the car and got in. His hands were shaking so badly it took a long time for him to get the key into the ignition, and when he finally started the engine and looked up she had disappeared inside the castle and shut the door.

He drove too fast, with the same kind of tense, focused clarity he felt in an ambush. He had an acute hyper-awareness of the smallest details—the digital dashboard statistics registering fuel consumption, the change in colour of the spreading bruise on his knuckles from red to purple to blue—but the miles were swallowed up without him being able to say whereabouts he was or for how long he'd been driving.

He stopped only once, but that was while he was still on the narrow Northumbrian roads not far from Alnburgh and the memory of Sophie's face was still clear and raw and painful. Not for the briefest split second had he been in danger of hitting her, but the way she'd flinched away from him and raised her hands in self-defence was enough to make the bile rise in the back of his throat. He pulled over, getting out of the car and filling his starved lungs with gulps of air before getting into the driver's seat again. He caught a glimpse of himself in the rear-view mirror, and his face was the face of a stranger. A stranger he didn't want to know.

The needle on the speedometer was almost vertical now, the motorway rushing past in an anonymous blur so that he felt a jolt of surprise when he read the name of the town to which he was headed on the exit sign that loomed ahead.

Leaving the motorway forced him out of his trancelike state. He hadn't bothered to programme the car's sat-nav, so had to concentrate on following signs to the hospital in which the unit to which Lewis had been transferred was situated. It wasn't easy. His mind refused to stay focused on the incomprehensible system of roundabouts and dual carriageways and kept being pulled back to what had happened earlier. Each time he replayed the scene in his head the self-loathing he felt increased.

Pulling up in the hospital car park, he took his mobile phone from the pocket of his jacket and dialled Alnburgh. In his head he could hear the phone shrilling through the portrait hall, shattering the thick silence of the library. Seconds ticked by. His bruised and swollen knuckles throbbed as he gripped the phone tightly.

And just when he was about to give up there was a click and a pause, and then Sophie's low, slightly breathless voice.

'Hello?'

Kit closed his eyes. Just hearing her say that one word drove back the demons and stilled the panic. He tipped his head back, desperately trying to find his own voice. When he did it was hoarse and cracked.

'Sophie, it's me.'

There was a pause. He pictured her face, seeing in his mind the two lines of anguish he knew would have appeared between her fine brows, the way she would be pressing her lips together to keep her emotions in check.

'Where are you?'

'I just got to the hospital.'

'Already? That was quick.'

Was it? He glanced at the dashboard clock and noticed absently she was right. 'I had to say sorry.'

'There's no need.' She said it quickly, in a low, miserable voice. 'It wasn't you…I…overreacted. I'm sorry.'

'Don't.' Hearing her blame herself for his behaviour was more than he could bear. 'Please. Don't take responsibility for my failings. You were right…' He paused, closing his eyes and massaging his forehead with his fingertips, as if he could rub away the memory of what he'd done.

'About what?'

'About what you said about my mother, and Ralph. I didn't want to hear it and I lost control. But I wouldn't have hit you, Sophie. Whatever else you think, I want you to believe that. I would *never* hurt you.'

There was a long silence.

'You've shut me out of your life, Kit. Nothing could hurt more than that.'

Sophie put the phone down and then stood back, staring at it. Her eyes were dry, but she knew that the tears were there inside her, and that when they came they would flow for a long, long time.

For a moment, when he'd said that she was right she'd thought—*hoped*—he'd rung to tell her he'd changed his mind. That he had to be with her, whatever. That what they had was stronger than anything else life could throw at them. That his love was unconditional.

But it wasn't.

He felt guilty for frightening her, that was all. He'd rung because he couldn't know that in the instant when he'd raised his fist it had triggered a memory, buried so long and so deep that the details had dimmed to an impressionistic blur, but which still brought the sour taste of terror into her mouth.

She picked up the bag at her feet and walked through to the long gallery, looking round at the unsmiling Fitzroys, the stuffed animal heads with their glassy eyes and rictus snarls for the last time. On impulse she put down her bag and opened the door to the dining room and switched on the light. The chrysanthemums stood where she had put them yesterday, when she'd thought that a candlelit dinner was all that was needed to cross the chasm between her and Kit.

She almost wanted to laugh at her own naiveté.

Without thinking, she found herself walking forwards until she was standing beneath the portrait of the woman with the roses in her hair and The Dark Star on her finger—a fellow outsider who had failed to fit in at Alnburgh and ended up paying the price with her life. Sophie raised her hand and looked down at the ring, remembering what Kit had said about refusing to sentence her to a slow death with him. She smoothed her thumb over the iridescent opal. Caring for him when he needed her wouldn't have killed her, but loving a man who held himself back from her might, in the end.

Very slowly she eased the ring off her finger and held it in her hand for a second. Her finger felt lighter without it. Empty. Then she put it on the mantelpiece, just below the portrait, and went out of the room.

It was time to move on again.

The specialist Army Rehabilitation Centre to which Lewis had been moved when he came out of Intensive Care was newly built and furnished in bright primary colours. Kit followed a pretty, plump nurse down a corridor that smelled of paint, to Lewis's room. She knocked and opened the door without waiting for an answer.

'There's someone here to see you.'

Through the open door Kit could see Lewis sitting in front of a television screen, the control for a games console in his hand. At the nurse's words his head snapped round, but the hope on his face vanished instantly when Kit walked past her into the room.

'Oh. It's you, sir,' he said sullenly, a blush stealing up his neck as he turned back to his game. 'What are you doing here?'

'I wanted to see you. To find out how you're doing. Is it OK if I sit down?'

Lewis nodded, but his gaze didn't move from the screen, which showed an animated railway line in grim, twilight colours, with a row of derelict-looking buildings behind it. Sitting on the edge of the bed, Kit rubbed his burning palms against his thighs and, averting his eyes, looked at Lewis instead.

He was a shadow of the boy who'd brought Kit coffee on that morning a few weeks ago and spilled most of it onto the sand in his haste and enthusiasm. He'd lost a lot of weight, and, with his hair shaved off and the scar where they'd operated to remove the bullet from his head still raw, he looked frail. As fragile as a child.

'You look well,' Kit lied with impressive calm, given the pickaxe of guilt lodged in his chest and the fact that his heart felt as if it had been fed through a mincing machine. 'A hell of a lot better than last time I saw you, anyway. How are you feeling?'

Lewis answered in a single monosyllabic word. It was a concise response, if not one that would usually be acceptable to a commanding officer. His eyes were fixed to the screen, where shadowy figures darted from buildings and jumped out of containers beside the railway line. Understanding the sentiment behind it all too well, Kit let the language go.

'Sorry to hear that. I spoke to Dr Randall. He says you've made incredible progress and shown a huge amount of courage. A lot of men wouldn't have pulled through at all, never mind as quickly and well as you have.'

Lewis's thumb pressed a red button on the control repeatedly and volleys of animated fire lit up the screen. Kit watched their red reflections in the dilated pupils of Lewis's unblinking eyes.

'I'm doing OK in that way,' he said dully. 'I need to get back to fitness. Back to how I was before.'

'You want to go back out there?'

'I dunno. I haven't decided yet. If things here don't work out…'

Lewis let the sentence trail off, but his thumb continued its rapid movement, annihilating the animated enemy.

'How's Kelly?'

A fireball filled the screen and Lewis's shoulders slumped.

'Dunno. Haven't seen her, have I? She doesn't like it here. Says hospitals freak her out.'

Mentally Kit cursed. There was a restless feeling building in the back of his head and a sweat had broken out on his forehead. 'That's a good incentive to get out of here, then.'

Lewis started the game again, his hands moving jerkily as he guided a figure in SAS fatigues at a run along a deserted street. 'That's what I thought, but now—I dunno. One of my mates told me she's seeing someone else. He works at the gym I used to go to.' Red spurts of gunfire erupted from a blank window and the figure on the screen fell to the ground. 'I can't blame her, can I? I mean, look at me.' Throwing the control down, he stood up, his eyes wild, his thin arms spread out. 'I'm pathetic. I can't even get dressed without help, never mind do fifty push-ups, and I know that was what she fancied about me in the first place. I was fit then, and now I'm… *nothing.*'

'Bullshit, Sapper.' Kit thanked seventeen years of rigorous army discipline for the ability to keep his voice clipped, curt, emotionless. 'You're a soldier who took several bullets

while doing a job that would make a gym instructor cry for
his mother. Probably the worst injury he's sustained in the
line of duty is a pulled muscle. You were shot at close range
by a semi-automatic rifle in the hands of a man who wanted
to kill you, and you're fighting back.'

As if in slow motion Lewis's face crumpled. Tears welled
in his eyes and spilled over his hollow, parchment-pale cheeks
as he sank back into his seat.

'I wanted to be a hero for her,' he sobbed, rubbing at his
eyes like a little child. 'All the time we were out there I was
thinking of her and the baby. I just wanted to make them
proud of me…and look what happened. I lost them instead.'

Kit got to his feet, desperately trying to keep his gaze
from straying back to the twitching figure of the soldier on
the screen. His hands felt as if they'd been dipped in acid that
was dissolving the flesh, burning up the nerves.

'You can't look at it that way. You're a lucky man. When
I last saw you the doctors weren't sure if the bullet had sev-
ered your spine or not; they weren't sure if you'd walk again.
You're back on your feet—you're going to be OK.'

Lewis lifted his tear-streaked face to look at him helplessly.

'So what? I'd rather be injured and have her than be walking around, trying to live a normal life without her.'

Kit had already opened his mouth to say something brisk
and acerbic in response, but nothing came out. Out of the corner of his eye he could see the game on the screen start over
again and he was unable to stop himself turning to watch the
figure moving down the street of its own accord this time as
snipers appeared on rooftops and windows.

'We don't choose what happens,' he said hoarsely. Blood
thrummed in his ears. 'You just have to make the best of
the hand you're dealt. You'll find someone who loves you,
no matter what. Someone you don't have to prove anything
to.' Forcing his gaze from the screen, he looked hollowly at
Lewis, trying to see him as he was now, here, rather than re-

membering the blood running down his face into the sand. Panic loomed, and automatically he thought of Sophie—her smile, her scent—to drive it back.

'You just have to be sure that when you find her, you're not stupid enough to push her away.'

Angrily Lewis swiped the tears from his cheeks. 'The trouble is I don't want anyone else. I just want her.'

Kit went to the door. 'Then don't let her go,' he said wearily. 'Fight for her.'

Out in the corridor he leaned against the wall and took a ragged breath.

'Kit?' He felt Randall's hand on his shoulder. 'Are you all right?'

It seemed that people were always asking him that these days, Kit thought, and he always came up with the same untruthful answer. But he'd run out of lies now. Raising his head, he looked Randall in the eye.

'Not really.' He held up his shaking hands and managed a bleak smile. 'Those tests I asked about when we spoke on the phone—what would they involve?'

Randall's expression stayed professionally blank as he glanced at Kit's hands. 'A variety of things—nothing too complicated. We can make a start on eliminating the obvious things straight away, if you want?'

Kit paused for a heartbeat, then nodded.

It felt as if he'd driven Sophie away already. He had nothing more to lose.

CHAPTER THIRTEEN

THE early-autumn dusk was already beginning to fall as Sophie slowed the Range Rover that had once belonged to Ralph Fitzroy and swung it into the potholed farm track.

It had been five years at least since she'd last visited, but she remembered every tree and gateway on the final bit of the journey. The tears that had remained unshed throughout the seemingly interminable drive from Alnburgh prickled at the backs of her eyes as she bounced across the field towards the cluster of ancient caravans and camper vans and pulled up alongside Rainbow's bus.

The painted flowers were peeling and a peace symbol over the back wheel had lost one of its three prongs so that it now looked ironically like the logo of an executive car manufacturer, but otherwise the place in which she'd grown up was pretty much unchanged. It even smelled the same, she noticed as she got out of the car and breathed in the scent of Calor gas, frying onions and wet grass.

On legs that felt as weak as a foal's from being in the car for so long, she walked round to the front of the bus and knocked. The windows, as always, were clouded with condensation, but through it she could see movement. The next moment Rainbow flung open the door, her faced wreathed in smiles.

'Summer—you're here!'

Her voice was warm and filled with pleasure, but not undue surprise. Emerging from a patchouli-and-lavender-scented hug, Sophie gave her mother a watery smile.

'You sound like you were expecting me.'

Ushering her in, Rainbow shrugged. Since Sophie had last seen her, her hair had grown past her shoulders and was now a rather beautiful shade of foxglove pink, darker at the ends so that it look as if it had been dip-dyed. She was wearing her usual collection of layered things—a long skirt with a long tunic top covered by a long loose cardigan, all in shades of indigo and purple.

'I was, in a way. I've been getting the Three of Cups a lot lately. It's the card of reunions, so naturally I've been thinking of you.' She gestured to the little table where her worn deck of tarot cards lay. 'Then this morning I got The Tower, so I suppose it's fair to say that I'm not surprised to see you.'

Very recently—like, a couple of days ago—Sophie would have given an inward sneer at all this. But not any more. Now she picked up the top card, which showed a high turret on a rock just like Kit's bedroom at Alnburgh. The sky behind it was black, lightning struck it and flames billowed from the windows, from where two human figures plummeted downwards.

'This is The Tower?' Sophie suppressed a shudder. 'Why did that make you think of me?'

'Well, it was the Cups that made me think of you, but once you were there in my mind The Tower told me all wasn't well.' Rainbow's eyes were the faded blue of summer skies and well-worn jeans, and Sophie saw concern in them now. 'It denotes pain—often coming like a lightning bolt out of the blue, shattering faith and belief. Though, of course,' she added hastily, 'it can be read in different ways...'

'That way is accurate enough for me,' said Sophie with an awkward little laugh.

Rainbow glanced at her, but only said, 'Why don't you sit

down? Have you eaten? Hilary made carrot and coriander soup and dropped some round for me earlier.'

'That sounds wonderful,' Sophie said gratefully, sinking down onto the sagging couch, suddenly aware that she was ravenous. As Rainbow set about lighting the gas and the little space was filled with the smell that made Sophie feel about eight years old again she looked around. The bus hadn't changed much, but the cheap nylon curtains she remembered had been replaced with pretty ones—a different printed cotton in each window—and there were bright patchwork cushions on the two couches. It looked nice, Sophie realised with a wrench. Homely.

'I've been away too long,' she said sadly. 'I've been a pretty rubbish daughter, haven't I?'

'Nonsense.' Briskly Rainbow moved the tarot cards and laid a spoon and a bright blue pottery bowl on the table. 'You know I've never held with all that family obligation stuff. You came back when you needed to, and that's what matters to me.'

'You're not hurt that I haven't been back for five years?'

'I think of you often, if that's what you mean,' said Rainbow, pouring thick soup into the bowl. 'But in a good way. You were always fiercely independent, even as a little girl. Self-contained. I knew you wouldn't want to stay here any longer than you had to, and that I had no right to make you feel you should.' She sat down opposite Sophie, her face serene. 'Living like this was my choice, but I always respected your right to make choices of your own.'

Sophie picked up her spoon. 'Why did you choose to live like this?'

'Well, I didn't choose it initially. It came about by accident, I suppose, because I ran away from an unhappy marriage.'

'To my father.' Sophie paused, a spoonful of soup halfway to her mouth, her mind going back to the moment when

Kit had brought his fist down on the car bonnet. 'He hit you, didn't he?'

Rainbow looked down at the table, tracing her finger over one of the many scars on its surface. 'I always wondered if you remembered anything about that time.'

'I didn't.' Until today. 'How old was I when we left?'

'Three.' Rainbow looked up at her then, her expression almost apologetic. 'He hit me in front of you once too often, you see, and I knew that if I didn't get out I'd be destroying your chances of a normal life as well as throwing away my own.'

'Oh, Mum…'

It slipped out instinctively, even though Sophie couldn't remember the last time she'd addressed Rainbow like that. Rainbow didn't seem to notice though. Or if she did, she didn't seem to mind.

'Well, everything happens for a reason.' She sighed. 'I'm not saying it wasn't horrible at the time, because it was and I wouldn't wish it on anyone, but without all that I'd never have ended up at the camp. I hadn't been planning to leave, but I went straight to the station, got on the first train that came and went as far as we could before the guard chucked us off for not having a ticket. Which turned out to be Newbury. There was a woman getting into a camper van outside the station and I asked her for directions to a B&B.' Propping her chin on her hand Rainbow smiled in reminiscence. 'It was Bridget—you remember her?'

'I remember.' During her adolescence Bridget was one of the only things that had actually made Sophie appreciate Rainbow, simply because Bridget was infinitely more embarrassing. Built like a Sherman tank, dressed in dungarees and army boots, Bridget had presided over the peace camp like a new-age sergeant-major in drag. Even Kit would probably have been intimidated by her.

But she couldn't let herself think about Kit.

'She took one look at my bruised face—and you—and she knew exactly what our situation was. And that was the moment my whole life changed.' Rainbow got up to switch on a lamp and pull the curtains shut against the encroaching night. 'We went back to the peace camp with her and all the women made us so welcome. They were such good people, who had a vision of a better world with no bombs or wars or violence. We changed our names and started a new life with them. And, well…' she shrugged '…you know the rest.'

Laying her spoon down in the empty bowl, Sophie nodded slowly. She knew, of course, but until now she hadn't really understood. The steel behind the peace-and-love; the courage and the camaraderie and the conviction that gave that small group of dispossessed women the strength to raise their kids and stick two fingers up to a society that hadn't protected them.

She'd been so quick to write her mother off as a daft, tree-hugging hippy, and distance herself from her alternative lifestyle and eccentric friends. Shame flooded her as she remembered the excuses she'd made about not having a big wedding. *My mother is not most mothers*, she'd said in a tone of deep scorn, implying that was a bad thing.

And it wasn't. It was good, because she had taught her to be strong and independent and not to put up with second best. And she had loved her. Unconditionally.

'Thank you,' she said quietly, reaching across the table and taking her mother's heavily ringed hand in hers.

Rainbow looked surprised. 'For what?'

'Everything. Being brave enough to do what you did. For encouraging me to go and live my own life. And for being here for me now, even after all this time.'

Getting to her feet, Rainbow took Sophie's bowl. 'I'll always be here for you,' she said comfortably, putting water in the kettle and lighting the gas again. 'I couldn't give you much in terms of material stuff when you were growing up, but I used to tell myself that the two things I could give you were roots and wings. You'll always have a home here, but part of loving someone is letting them go.'

And it reminded her so much of Kit that to her horror Sophie felt her eyes suddenly filling with tears. 'Is it?' she said with a sob. 'But what if they don't want to go? What if they want to stay and face things alongside you?'

'Oh, sweetheart…' Rainbow's face creased into lines of compassion as she came forward and took Sophie into her arms. 'I knew something was wrong. What happened? Tell me all about it.'

And so, as the tears slid silently down her cheeks, Sophie did.

The box of tissues Rainbow had put on the table was almost empty by the time Sophie had finished, as was the bottle of Rainbow's damson gin, which had been brought out instead of herbal tea, in honour of the crisis. Sophie looked at her mother through eyes that were swollen with crying and managed a lopsided smile.

'When he asked me to marry him I thought I'd stumbled into the happy-ever-after part of the story. I never imagined there was going to be a sequel.'

Frowning, Rainbow shared the last of the gin between the two mugs in front of them. 'And you think all this means he doesn't love you?' she asked carefully.

'Not enough.' Sophie dropped her head into her hands. 'If he did he'd know that I'd just want to be there for him, *with* him.'

There was a little pause, during which the only sound was the spluttering hiss of the gas and a cow mooing mournfully in a distant field. 'Or it could mean he loves you more than you can possibly understand,' Rainbow suggested gently. 'Enough to want you to be happy, and to sacrifice his own interests to give you that chance. Enough to give you your freedom.'

Shredding a tissue between listless fingers, Sophie remembered what he'd said that morning. *You're the most amazing, vibrant person I've ever met... I won't condemn you to a life of watching me die by degrees. It would be like burying you alive.*

'But what if I don't want to be free?' she moaned. 'What if I just want to be with him?'

Rainbow leaned forwards and took her hands. 'That's the thing about loving someone.' Her eyes were full of tenderness but her voice was firm. 'It's not just about what *you* want any more. It's about what's best for both of you. He loves you enough to give you your freedom, and now you have to do the same for him. You have to trust him to make his own decisions, and respect them.'

'But it's so hard.' Sophie gasped, closing her eyes. In the darkness behind her throbbing eyelids she saw Kit's face and felt as if her heart had been split in two.

Rainbow's grip on her hands tightened. 'I know. But have faith. Everything happens for a reason, remember. If it's meant to be, it will be. If he loves you, you'll know.'

Opening her eyes, Sophie looked at her mother through a fog of despair. 'How?'

Rainbow gave her a bittersweet smile. 'Ah, now that I can't tell you. I guess you just have to wait for a sign.'

Kit sat in the hospital waiting room, beneath a fluorescent strip light that flickered unnervingly and emitted a persistent, low-frequency buzz. He'd been there for a long time and had become intimately acquainted with the arrangement of fake flowers on the table in the corner, and the covers of the women's magazines, showing pictures of tanned blondes with wide, blue-white smiles and vacant eyes.

For the hundredth time he picked up his phone and dialled, lifting it listlessly to his ear. The mobile reception at Alnburgh was virtually non-existent so he tried the castle's landline first, letting it ring on and on and on to make sure that Sophie had enough time to get to it, whatever she was doing. If she was there. But there was a part of him that knew with a cold, clear certainty that she wasn't.

She had told him that it was over if he didn't change his mind. She had given him the time to reconsider what he'd said, and the chance to take it back, but he'd refused to think about it, or to talk to her. Instead he'd lost his temper.

Well, he'd had plenty of chances to think about it now. Lying completely still in an MRI scanner tube for over an hour there was nothing to do *but* think. No alternative but to confront his utter stupidity.

With sudden impatience he cut the call to Alnburgh and dialled Sophie's mobile instead, sending up a silent, desperate prayer that this time she would pick up. Maybe before she'd been driving and unable to answer, but now…

'Kit—there you are. I'm so sorry to keep you hanging on like this.' Randall appeared round the corner, jolting him out of his private despair. He looked like hell—grey-faced and exhausted, and Kit noticed that there were splashes of blood on his shirt. 'It's been a long afternoon. We had another Medical Evacuation case. Landmine. Anyway, come into my office and we can talk.'

He was already striding down the corridor. Getting stiffly to his feet, Kit had little choice but to follow him.

'How is he? The medevac case?'

Shutting the door to his office, Randall visibly slumped. 'Well, the ones that get sent to me are never in a good way,' he said wearily, sinking into a chair behind a desk stacked high with skyscrapers of paper. 'But he's here and he's alive, which is a start. The physical damage is only part of it though. I can patch him up and send him home, but the mental effects of combat are a lot harder to sort out. Tell me, Kit…' he looked speculatively across the paper landscape, gesturing to Kit to take a seat '…how much do you know about PTSD?'

Kit stayed standing. 'Post-Traumatic Stress Disorder? I've been in the army long enough to know plenty of soldiers who've suffered it, though I haven't seen much of it firsthand since it only usually becomes apparent after they're home.' There was a little pause, and then he said, 'Sorry, Randall, but at the risk of sounding rude I really need to be going…'

Randall smiled ruefully and picked up a buff-coloured file from on top of one of the piles. 'Of course. You've been here quite long enough and you just want to know what the tests have shown up and get out of here.'

A kick of adrenaline squirted through Kit's body, like a mini-electric shock. 'You have the results already?'

'Most of them.' Randall flipped the file open and began to flick through the pages inside. 'The bloods take a little while to come back from the lab, but I have the MRI and electro-myography results…'

Kit turned away for a moment and took a deep breath. His heart was banging against his ribs.

'So—' Randall began.

'I don't want to know,' Kit cut him off, his voice low but utterly calm. 'Not yet.'

Randall looked up. His face was a picture of surprise and confusion.

'I know it's been hard for you to confront this, Kit, but—'

'It was.' Kit took two paces across the room, which brought him up against a filing cabinet where he turned and paced back again. 'But I'm bloody glad I did because it made me confront other things too, and realise how stupid I've been.' Finding himself back at the filing cabinet, he leaned his elbows on top of it and dropped his head into his hands. 'God, Randall, I've made such a mess of everything I can't tell you,' he moaned.

'You could try, if it would help?'

Kit's laugh was edged with desolation. 'Thanks, but there's no time. I need to find her and try to put things right before it's too late.'

'Ah.' Carefully Randall shut the file and put it back amongst the others. 'I thought there must be a woman involved somewhere.'

'"Somewhere" just about sums it up. I think she's left Alnburgh and I don't have the faintest bloody idea where she would have gone. And I have to find her before I know the results of these tests so I can stand in front of her and tell her, honestly, that Lewis was right. I'd rather have one year to live and spend it with her than have fifty years on my own.'

Randall rocked back in his chair, his expression unreadable. 'Does she have a mobile phone?'

'I've tried that.' Kit clenched his fists against his temples, only just managing to stop himself from snapping at the obviousness of the suggestion. 'She's not answering.'

'But it's switched on?' Randall said blandly. 'In that case, may I suggest that you make a quick call to the boys in the Signals Corps?' He gave Kit a conspiratorial smile. 'Strictly speaking I suppose it's not quite life or death, but…'

'Thanks, Randall.' Kit straightened up, a thin ray of hope breaking through the despair in his head. 'It certainly feels like it.'

CHAPTER FOURTEEN

'TEA, sweetheart.'

Sophie opened her eyes, only just managing to clamp back the groan of irritation at being woken. She didn't want to wake up. She didn't want to face the first day of her new Kit-free life, and all the implications that involved. Most immediately, she did not want a cup of Rainbow's revolting herbal tea.

'Thanks,' she muttered, in a way that was meant to convey a desire to be left alone.

'It's a beautiful morning,' Rainbow remarked calmly as she worked her way along the length of the upper deck, pulling back the curtains. 'How are you feeling today?'

'Not great.'

Sophie rolled onto her front and buried her face in the pillow. Her eyes hurt with crying, her back hurt from all the hours she'd spent driving yesterday and her heart hurt from knowing that she'd walked away from the only man she'd ever loved. The only man she ever would love, even if she lived to be a hundred, in a town full of handsome, single, charming men.

'That's understandable,' Rainbow said sympathetically, 'but just take a look at this beautiful view and you'll feel much better.'

'I doubt it.'

'Really, you can't fail to be cheered up by what's out here.

It's one of those perfect, crisp autumn mornings. The sun is up, the dew is sparkling on the grass…'

Sophie was seriously tempted to swear, but she bit it back. Her mother's relentless positivity might be completely inappropriate, but Sophie admired her for it. It was what had got her through her own grim situation and helped her to start again. She might have to start taking a few tips from Rainbow.

'…there isn't a *single* cloud in the sky…'

Reluctantly Sophie sat up, pulling back the curtain behind her bed and screwing up her face against the brightness outside. It was so dazzling that for a moment she thought…

'…and, look, there's an extremely expensive-looking black sports car parked in the field. You don't get many of those round here.'

For a second Sophie could only gape stupidly. She looked from the car to her mother and back again, to check that she hadn't imagined it. And then she looked back at Rainbow again.

Her eyes danced. 'I said you had to wait for a sign. And, look, there it is.'

It was a beautiful morning; Rainbow was right about that just as she'd been right about so much else. Jumping down from the bus, Sophie put on her mother's purple wellington boots and walked across the field towards Kit's car.

Her heart was pounding, hope beating against caution as she stepped through the long, wet grass, listening to the sound of birdsong and the heavy rasp of her own breath. The sun was glinting on the windscreen of the car, but as she got closer she could see through the glare. The driver's seat was reclined and Kit was in it, his head to one side. He was asleep.

Love hit her like a tidal wave, knocking the air from her lungs. In that instant she wanted nothing more than to run to the car, pull open the door and kiss his closed eyelids, his beautiful mouth, and tell him that she knew how stupid she'd been. But her mother's words still echoed in her ears. Loving someone wasn't about what you wanted any more. It was about what was best for both of you. And so she stood, perfectly still, in the middle of the field for a moment before turning round and beginning to walk very slowly away.

She was almost back at the bus when she heard the car door slam behind her.

'Sophie!'

She spun round. He had got out of the car, and was coming towards her with quick, angry strides, shielding his eyes from the sun. Sophie's heart turned over. For a moment she didn't move, but it was as if she were being pulled towards him by invisible forces. They both slowed and halted a few feet apart, gazing at each other in a mixture of fear and wonderment.

'I wasn't going to wake you,' she said awkwardly, tearing her eyes away. 'I wanted to, but...'

He gave an impatient jerk of his head. The morning sun shining in his face showed up his grey pallor, the shadows of exhaustion beneath his eyes. 'I didn't mean to fall asleep. I drove all night.'

Frowning, Sophie wrapped her arms across her chest. 'But how did you know I was here?'

'I pulled strings in the Signals Corps.' Kit sighed, dragging a hand through his untidy hair. 'They traced your phone to an area of about eight square miles. Once I was here the rest was guesswork.'

That didn't begin to convey the frustration of the last twelve hours, or the bone-deep tiredness that had ached through him as he came up against another dead end, or turned around after taking the hundredth wrong turning. He had found it just as the sun was rising over the downs and knew he'd arrived at the right place by the large Routemaster bus standing incongruously in the middle of the field. In its way it was as much of a beacon in the surrounding country-

side as Alnburgh, and the fact that it was painted with flowers and peace symbols made it doubly obvious that this was
Sophie's childhood home.

'I'm sorry,' he said wearily. The sun was shining in his
eyes, surrounding her with an aura of gold but making it impossible to read her expression or see anything beyond the
length of her bare legs and the flaming glory of her hair. 'I
had to talk to you, and when you didn't pick up the phone
at Alnburgh I knew you must have left. I tried your mobile,
but...' He trailed off, knowing that he couldn't justify what
he'd done. Looking away, he briefly covered his face with his
hand. 'You'd probably be within your rights to press charges
if you didn't want to be found.'

'I did,' she whispered, so softly that he wasn't sure if he'd
heard properly. 'I'm so sorry, Kit,' she went on, taking a step
towards him so he could see her face clearly for the first time.
'I had no right to lay down rules and issue ultimatums. If
you're ill, you have to deal with it in your own way. I'll respect and support you in whatever you decide.'

Her lips were bee-stung and beautiful, her eyes glittering
with fierce tears. It took every atom of will power Kit pos-
sessed to resist the need to close the remaining distance between them and kiss her until the sun went down again. He
stood his ground, gazing at her with eyes that felt as if they
were being pricked by a thousand hot needles.

'I had the test,' he rasped, then gave a painful, twisted
smile. 'In fact, I had a lot of tests. All yesterday afternoon—
electrodes and wires and needles and scans.'

She took a tiny gasping breath, as if she'd touched something hot. 'And—what did they show?'

He hesitated, gritting his teeth as he struggled to keep his
voice from cracking. 'They showed that whatever's wrong
with me could never be as bad as losing you. Hour after hour
all I wanted to do was tear off the wires and walk out of there

to find you and confront the thing that scares me more than anything.'

'Which is?'

Kit closed his eyes. His hands were clenched into fists at his sides. 'Being without you.'

He heard the soft sigh of the grass as she came towards him and the next thing he knew she had taken his face between her hands. Her kiss was infinitely tender, but also full of strength and certainty, and before he could stop himself he was kissing her back, his hands sliding into the warm silk of her hair as his tired body throbbed and sang at her nearness. When they parted his face was wet with her tears.

She gazed up at him, dazed and pained and breathless. 'All my life I've been trying to distance myself from who I really am and where I came from,' she whispered, 'but when I came back here yesterday I saw straight away how...*irrelevant* all that is.' She glanced towards the painted bus and the group of camper vans behind it. 'This is my past and I'm not ashamed of it any more. But the present and the future are what really matter now.' She paused, a flicker of pain crossing her face as the tears welled and fell. 'I love you, Kit,' she said, reaching up to touch his cheek. 'That's who I am. It's in my heart, my blood, my brain, and nothing—*nothing*—can take it away.'

Kit raised his hand, capturing hers against his face and holding it there. 'I don't know if I have Leo's condition or not,' he said hoarsely. 'I wouldn't let them tell me until I'd told you that I'll love you whatever the outcome.' He took a breath, summoning the strength and courage to be completely honest. 'When I found out about Leo, I was so terrified by the thought of being dependent on you that I pushed you away. What I didn't take into account was the fact that it's too late.' He shook his head helplessly. 'I'm there already.'

Reaching up, Sophie hooked a hand round the back of his neck and pulled his head down so she could kiss him again.

'We're there together,' she murmured in the second before their lips met.

When they went into the bus a little while later, Rainbow was sitting at the table, eating toast and turning over cards. She smiled up at Kit, completely at ease, as if she'd been expecting him too.

'Hi, I'm Rainbow, Sophie's mum.'

Sophie realised it was the first time her mother had called her by her proper name—her original name—maybe since the night she'd got on that train to Newbury.

'I'm Kit.'

He bent to kiss her cheek, putting one hand lightly on her shoulder and making it look like the most natural thing in the world. Her cheeks were a slightly lighter shade of pink than her hair when he straightened up again. Sophie had never seen her mother blush before.

She finished the last of her toast quickly and stood up. 'I was just going to, er…return the bowl that soup came in to Hilary, actually, so if you'll excuse me…' Brushing the crumbs from her fingers, she picked up the cards and headed for the door. 'She wanted me to do a reading for her so I might be…you know, a while…'

Sophie waited until Rainbow had closed the door and begun to hurry across the grass before letting out a snort of laughter. 'My mother isn't the most subtle person you'll ever meet. She clearly thinks we're about to rip each other's clothes off in an orgy of uncontrollable lust.'

Kit trailed a finger lazily down her cheek.

'It's a tempting idea…'

Ripples of desire shimmered up Sophie's spine, but she caught hold of his hand and pulled it away. 'Later,' she said huskily, smiling up into his eyes. 'Phone call first.'

Kit gave a rueful smile. 'OK, OK… Any chance of some coffee?'

'You'll be lucky.' Sophie laughed, opening the doors of the little row of cupboards above the sink. 'Herbal tea in various flavours of grass is the house speciality here.'

Kit looked around. 'I like it,' he said slowly. 'Not the herbal tea perhaps, but the bus. I like it a lot.'

Sophie stretched up to reach into the back of the last cupboard. 'I suppose it *is* kind of cool…'

She gave a squeal as Kit's hands closed around her waist. His lips brushed the side of her neck, making goosebumps of pleasure rise on her arms.

'And a lot more convenient for hauling you off to bed than Alnburgh,' he murmured, kissing her ear lobe and reducing her to a quivering ache of desire.

She twisted around in his arms, so that she was facing him and could kiss him back, properly. As their mouths met she slid her hands into the back pockets of his jeans and pulled out his mobile phone. Laughing, slightly breathless from the kiss, she broke away and held it up.

'Nice try,' she gasped, tossing it to him. 'Now…phone.'

She lit the gas and set the kettle on the stove, unscrewing the lid of a pretty ancient-looking jar of instant coffee she'd discovered hidden by a packet of flaxseed and a large jar of Black Cohosh capsules. Behind her, Kit sat down at the table and dialled. Then, laying down the phone in the centre of the table he activated the speaker function so that the ringtone echoed through the small space. Sophie found she was holding her breath as a brisk female voice answered. Quickly she took the kettle off the boil before its wheezing whistle could build into a full-blown shriek. A male voice came on the line.

'Mike Randall.'

'Morning, Randall, it's Kit Fitzroy.'

'Kit—I was just thinking about you.' The coffee smelled

surprisingly good as Sophie poured hot water onto it. 'Do I gather you found her, then?'

'How did you know?'

'It's obvious from your voice. You're smiling.'

Sophie carried the mugs of coffee over and set them on the table. 'OK. I found her,' Kit admitted, catching her hand and holding it tightly. 'Thanks to you. She's right here, and I'm ready to hear whatever it is you have to tell me.'

Their gazes locked as Sophie sat down in the seat opposite. Time seemed to stand still and the rest of the world melt away so that there were just the two of them in the warm, sunlit space. And the innocuous-looking mobile phone on the table between them, through which they were about to discover their future.

'Thank goodness for that.' Randall's tone was dry, and in the background they could hear the rustle of paper as he opened a file. Kit's face was ashen but completely without expression. His silver gaze held hers, unblinking. Unflinching.

'Look, I won't beat about the bush, Kit,' Randall said, more certainly now. 'It's not Motor Neurone Disease. All the tests show that there's no sign of any kind of neuromuscular breakdown—in fact, it's obvious that your muscle function is way above average.'

Sophie couldn't stop a little gasping cry escaping her—partly from the momentary increase in the pressure of Kit's grip on her hand, partly as the breath she had been holding escaped her in a rush. Kit's head rocked back for a second as if against a physical blow.

'That's good,' he said in a voice that was taut with suppressed emotion. His eyes found Sophie's again, a slow smile dawning in their luminous depths, like the sun rising over the field outside. 'You're not about to tell me that it's something just as sinister, are you?'

There was a pause.

'No,' Randall said. 'But remember yesterday I asked you about Post-Traumatic Stress Disorder?'

Sophie felt the jolt that went through Kit's body in the moment before he let go of her hand. 'You're not saying you think that's what this is?' he said sharply, turning away from her and looking out of the window. 'I thought that was a mental condition?'

'It is, largely.' Randall's voice was carefully neutral. 'PTSD is a complex condition that can result in a wide range of symptoms, from difficulty sleeping to hyper-vigilance, paranoia, flashbacks, bursts of uncontrollable anger… Does any of that sound familiar?'

Beyond the smeared glass the bright morning blurred and darkened. Kit's mind raced. He could feel the sweat break out on his forehead as the familiar numbness invaded his fingers and burned across his palms. He opened his mouth to deny it, but the razor wire tightened around his throat and the words wouldn't come.

'Yes.' It was Sophie who broke the silence, her voice quiet and certain. She reached across and put her hand to his cheek, very gently bringing his face round towards her. 'That was what happened in Morocco, wasn't it?' she said softly. 'In the souk. You had a flashback, didn't you?'

There was nowhere left to hide, no more ammunition with which he could fight. He felt as if he'd come to the end of a long stand-off, and there was nothing left for him to do but walk out into the open with his hands in the air.

'Yes.' His throat felt as if it were full of sand. Sophie's gaze was green and cool, as soothing as deep shade on a hot day, but he couldn't quite let himself slip into it yet. 'But what about my hands? You're saying it's all in my mind, aren't you?'

Randall sighed. 'No. I'm saying the numbness and lack of co-ordination could be an extreme stress response in someone who's been through a lot. More than one person can deal with alone.' Opposite, Sophie stood up and walked silently around the table, taking his face between her hands. 'I've talked to soldiers who've served under you, Kit,' Randall continued, his voice subdued. 'I know how much you take on yourself in order to spare your men. It's tough out there at the best of times, and you've seen more than your fair share of the worst of times.' Sophie's eyes didn't leave his. With infinite tenderness she bent her head and kissed his lips; sweetly, softly. 'No one can do that indefinitely without it having some effect,' Randall went on, oblivious, as Kit stumbled to his feet, wrapping his arms around Sophie, holding her hard against his body and kissing her back as if his life depended on it. 'My guess is you dealt with it before by simply blocking out all emotion, but now—' Randall broke off with a short, wistful laugh. 'Well, welcome to the human race, Major Fitzroy.'

Slowly, reluctantly, Kit took his mouth from Sophie's, but they stayed close together, their foreheads touching, their gazes locked.

'OK, I take the point,' Kit said harshly. 'So what now?'

'Talking helps,' Randall replied from the other end of the phone. 'Not bottling up emotion.'

Kit gave a lopsided smile as Sophie brushed a tear from his cheek with her thumb. 'I'm onto it.'

'Often just getting some of the memories out into the open can help the mind to process them and stop the cycle,' Randall said, above the sound of shuffling papers. 'I can find out the numbers of people who can help, if you'd like…'

'Thanks, Randall,' Kit said in a low voice, reaching for the phone. 'But you already did that, remember? I owe you.'

'Not at all. I'm just doing my job, like you were just doing yours. You can invite me to the wedding though. I'd like to meet this wonderful girl.'

'You're on.'

Ending the call, Kit raised his head and looked at Sophie.

He felt inexpressibly tired, as if he'd been walking for days and was now in sight of home.

'So, it looks like you're stuck with me for the next fifty years at least,' he said in a voice that was gruff with love, smoothing a strand of hair back from her face.

She closed her eyes briefly. 'Thank God for that.' A shadow of anguish flickered across her face, but then she opened her eyes and smiled and it was gone. 'Now could we possibly go to bed?'

Kit shook his head, picking up his phone again and scrolling through the numbers. 'Not yet. I have one more call to make first. Estate business.'

'Kit... How could you...?' Sophie protested as the sound of the dialling tone rang out again. Laughing, she made a move to grab the phone from him and he held it out of her reach, sliding a hand up her bare thigh beneath the shirt as she jumped to grab it. She let out a squeal at exactly the same moment that a bored voice came on the other end of the line.

'Hello, Northumbrian Holidays, how can I help?'

Collapsing back against the worktop, Sophie clamped a hand over her mouth to stifle her laughter. Kit struggled to make his tone businesslike, and take his thoughts off how outrageously beautiful and sexy she was.

'It's Kit Fitzroy. I'm phoning with regard to Castle Farm at Alnburgh.'

Sophie's eyes widened.

'Oh, yes, Lord Fitzroy.' The voice became noticeably warmer and more interested. 'Is there a problem?'

'I'm afraid so,' Kit said gravely. 'Due to circumstances... entirely beyond my control, I'm sorry to say the farmhouse is going to be unavailable for rent. With immediate effect. Obviously anyone with existing bookings will be generously compensated.'

Sophie dropped her hand. Her mouth was open and all

traces of laughter had left her face. In its place was an expression of naked longing and deep, unstinting love.

'Oh, dear,' sighed the bored woman on the other end of the phone. 'That's most unfortunate. At least it's the end of the season, I suppose. Can I ask how long you expect it to be unavailable for?'

Kit touched Sophie's lips with his fingertips, smiling into her eyes.

'For ever,' he said.

EPILOGUE

THE first fat flakes of snow were just beginning to fall from an iron-grey sky as the Routemaster bus lumbered through Alnburgh village. In spite of the cold the road to the church was lined with people, all eager to catch a glimpse of the bride, and the crowd burst into a round of spontaneous applause as the bus swung into the churchyard and shuddered to a halt in a cloud of diesel fumes.

As she peered out into the gloom of the winter afternoon a lump came to Sophie's throat.

'So much for a small wedding,' she joked weakly. The crowd was full of familiar faces. Sophie spotted Mrs Watts and the landlady of The King's Arms, their cheeks flushed with cold and excitement, and she felt unbearably touched.

Rainbow climbed out of the driver's seat, looking strikingly lovely in a long, black and fabulously Gothic fitted coat that skimmed her ankles and showed off her beautiful hair.

'Are you ready?'

Sophie picked up her bouquet of dark red roses. 'Ready? Are you kidding? I can't wait. I know it's tradition for the bride and groom not to see each other on their wedding day, but I feel like I've been apart from Kit for ever. I just want to get the service bit over so I can talk to him.'

Juliet Fitzroy got up from her seat and adjusted the simple coronet of ivy leaves that rested on top of Sophie's cascade of auburn hair—still slightly paint-spattered from all the decorating she'd been doing at the farmhouse. As Sophie's matron of honour, Juliet was wearing a little fitted shift dress of dark green silk, simple and elegant.

'You've got the rest of your lives to talk.' She smiled fondly and touched Sophie's cheek. 'Enjoy every minute of this. It's your day.'

Rainbow shook her head mutely, her blue eyes bright with tears.

'And you look so beautiful. I'm so—' She broke off, pressing her fingers to her mouth. Juliet put a hand on her arm and a look of empathy passed between them.

'Your mother is proud of you, and so am I,' she said in her grave, husky voice that contained so many echoes of Kit's. 'You deserve to be so happy, my darling.'

'Thank you.' Determined not to cry and smudge her mascara, Sophie looked down at her hands and blinked fiercely. The Dark Star glistened on her finger, soon to be joined by a plain gold band.

'You're quite sure opals aren't unlucky?' she asked one last time.

'Absolutely and completely.' Rainbow sniffed stoically. 'The old wives' tale is that they're unlucky *unless* it's your birthstone, which it is. But in crystal healing black opals are thought to release fear and bring a sense of empowerment. They're also associated with strong sexual attraction.'

Sophie laughed, and the tiny shard of hope lodged in her heart twisted a little. The desire between her and Kit burned as fiercely as ever, only now it was accompanied by conversations that carried on late into the night in which they often talked about their hopes for the future. For a family. She wasn't sure yet, and she'd been disappointed before, but...

Maybe.

Rainbow got out of the bus first, holding up her hand to help her daughter down. Sophie's dress was a narrow column of silk, overlaid with gossamer-fine lace that glittered with tiny beads. It was so narrow that it made the steps of the bus difficult to manage. Holding Rainbow's hand, she hoisted her skirt up and jumped down.

The little crowd of well-wishers erupted into a chorus of whoops and cheers and the sound carried into the candlelit church, sending a ripple of excitement through the assembled congregation. At the front of the church Kit turned to Jasper. In contrast to Jasper's LA tan, his face was almost as white as the starched collar of his shirt and a muscle was flickering in his cheek. 'What's happening?' he said tersely. 'I heard them arrive ages ago. You don't think she's having second thoughts, do you?'

Suppressing a smile, Jasper shrugged nonchalantly. This new, human side to his previously marble-hearted brother hadn't yet lost the power to surprise and amuse him. 'She might have,' he said with mock concern. 'She wasn't very sure she wanted to marry you.'

Muttering a curse, Kit made to set off back up the aisle. 'I'm going to see if she's all right.'

Jasper lunged after him and blocked his way. 'Kit, don't be an ass, and don't make me have to try and restrain you because we both know I couldn't.' He rolled his eyes in exasperation. 'I knew I should have opted to be Sophie's bridesmaid instead.'

Sidestepping him, Kit went over to one of the many men in military uniform on the Fitzroy side of the church.

'Lewis, go and check everything's OK outside, would you?'

'No problem.' Lewis handed his baby son back to his new wife sitting in the pew beside him and hurried up the aisle with much of his old assurance. He was back a moment later, grinning broadly and sticking his thumbs up.

A hushed murmur travelled forwards from the back of the church.

Sophie was standing in the doorway. She wore no veil and

there were snowflakes in her hair, sparkling like tiny diamonds on her crown of ivy leaves.

Kit's heart stopped and in that instant all the tension fell away from him. As she stepped forwards the congregation fell silent. There was no organ music, no bridal march, just a group of Rainbow's friends high up in the gallery at the back of the church playing an old and hauntingly beautiful folk tune called 'The South Wind' on a tin whistle, a guitar and a violin.

And Sophie, laughing and crying, one hand in Rainbow's, the other in Juliet's, walking towards him. She looked strong, happy and so beautiful that Kit wasn't the only one whose eyes were suddenly smarting with tears.

He couldn't wait. Leaving a resigned Jasper at the altar, he strode towards her and, meeting her halfway along the aisle, gathered her into his arms. Sliding his hands into her gleaming hair, he kissed her, on and on.

The vicar sighed and raised his eyes to heaven.

'I hadn't got to that bit yet.'

* * * * *

CLASSIC

Quintessential, modern love stories
that are romance at its finest.

You can find more information on upcoming Harlequin® titles,
free excerpts and more at www.HarlequinInsideRomance.com.

HPCNM0112

REQUEST YOUR
FREE BOOKS!

 Harlequin *Presents*

 PASSION GUARANTEED SEDUCTION

2 FREE NOVELS PLUS
2 FREE GIFTS!

YES! Please send me 2 FREE Harlequin Presents® novels and my 2 FREE gifts (gifts are worth about $10). After receiving them, if I don't wish to receive any more books, I can return the shipping statement marked "cancel." If I don't cancel, I will receive 6 brand-new novels every month and be billed just $4.30 per book in the U.S. or $4.99 per book in Canada. That's a saving of at least 14% off the cover price! It's quite a bargain! Shipping and handling is just 50¢ per book in the U.S. and 75¢ per book in Canada.* I understand that accepting the 2 free books and gifts places me under no obligation to buy anything. I can always return a shipment and cancel at any time. Even if I never buy another book, the two free books and gifts are mine to keep forever. 106/306 HDN FERQ

Name _____ (PLEASE PRINT)

Address _____ Apt. #

City _____ State/Prov. _____ Zip/Postal Code

Signature (if under 18, a parent or guardian must sign)

Mail to the Reader Service:
IN U.S.A.: P.O. Box 1867, Buffalo, NY 14240-1867
IN CANADA: P.O. Box 609, Fort Erie, Ontario L2A 5X3

Not valid for current subscribers to Harlequin Presents books.

**Are you a current subscriber to Harlequin Presents books
and want to receive the larger-print edition?
Call 1-800-873-8635 or visit www.ReaderService.com.**

* Terms and prices subject to change without notice. Prices do not include applicable taxes. Sales tax applicable in N.Y. Canadian residents will be charged applicable taxes. Offer not valid in Quebec. This offer is limited to one order per household. All orders subject to credit approval. Credit or debit balances in a customer's account(s) may be offset by any other outstanding balance owed by or to the customer. Please allow 4 to 6 weeks for delivery. Offer available while quantities last.

Your Privacy—The Reader Service is committed to protecting your privacy. Our Privacy Policy is available online at www.ReaderService.com or upon request from the Reader Service.

We make a portion of our mailing list available to reputable third parties that offer products we believe may interest you. If you prefer that we not exchange your name with third parties, or if you wish to clarify or modify your communication preferences, please visit us at www.ReaderService.com/consumerschoice or write to us at Reader Service Preference Service, P.O. Box 9062, Buffalo, NY 14269. Include your complete name and address.

HPI1B

USA TODAY bestselling author

Sarah Morgan

brings readers another enchanting story

ONCE A FERRARA
WIFE...

When Laurel Ferrara is summoned back to Sicily
by her estranged husband, billionaire
Cristiano Ferrara, Laurel knows things are about
to heat up. And Cristiano's power is a potent
reminder of his Sicilian dynasty's unbreakable rule:
once a Ferrara wife, always a Ferrara wife....

Sparks fly this February

Louisa Morgan loves being around children.
So when she has the opportunity to tutor bedridden Ellie,
she's determined to bring joy back into the motherless
girl's world. Can she also help Ellie's father open his
heart again? Read on for a sneak peek of

THE COWBOY FATHER

by Linda Ford,
available February 2012 from Love Inspired Historical.

Why had Louisa thought she could do this job? A bubble of self-pity whispered she was totally useless, but Louisa ignored it. She wasn't useless. She could help Ellie if the child allowed it.

Emmet walked her out, waiting until they were out of earshot to speak. "I sense you and Ellie are not getting along."

"Ellie has lost her freedom. On top of that, everything is new. Familiar things are gone. Her only defense is to exert what little independence she has left. I believe she will soon tire of it and find there are more enjoyable ways to pass the time."

He looked doubtful. Louisa feared he would tell her not to return. But after several seconds' consideration, he sighed heavily. "You're right about one thing. She's lost everything. She can hardly be blamed for feeling out of sorts."

"She hasn't lost everything, though." Her words were quiet, coming from a place full of certainty that Emmet was more than enough for this child. "She has you."

"She'll always have me. As long as I live." He clenched his fists. "And I fully intend to raise her in such a way that even if something happened to me, she would never feel like I was gone. I'd be in her thoughts and in her actions every day."

Peace filled Louisa. "Exactly what my father did."

Their gazes connected, forged a single thought about fathers and daughters...how each needed the other. How sweet the relationship was.

Louisa tipped her head away first. "I'll see you tomorrow."

Emmet nodded. "Until tomorrow then."

She climbed behind the wheel of their automobile and turned toward home. She admired Emmet's devotion to his child. It reminded her of the love her own father had lavished on Louisa and her sisters. Louisa smiled as fond memories of her father filled her thoughts. Ellie was a fortunate child to know such love.

Louisa understands what both father and daughter are going through. Will her compassion help them heal—and form a new family? Find out in
THE COWBOY FATHER
by Linda Ford, available February 14, 2012.

Love Inspired Books celebrates 15 years of inspirational romance in 2012! February puts the spotlight on Love Inspired Historical, with each book celebrating family and the special place it has in our hearts. Be sure to pick up all four Love Inspired Historical stories, available February 14, wherever books are sold.

Discover a touching new trilogy from
USA TODAY bestselling author

Janice Kay Johnson

Between Love and Duty

As the eldest brother of three, Duncan MacLachlan
is used to being in control and maintaining an
emotional distance; as a police captain it's his job.
But when he meets Jane Brooks, Duncan soon finds
his control slipping away. Together, they fight for a
young boy's future, and soon Duncan finds himself
hoping to build a future with Jane.

Available February 2012

From Father to Son
(March 2012)

The Call of Bravery
(April 2012)

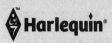
Harlequin®

nocturne™

NEW YORK TIMES AND *USA TODAY*
BESTSELLING AUTHOR

RACHEL LEE

captivates with another installment of

The Claiming

When Yvonne Dupuis gets a creepy sensation that
someone is watching her, waiting in the shadows,
she turns to Messenger Investigations and finds herself
under the protection of vampire Creed Preston.
His hunger for her is extreme, but with evil lurking
at every turn Creed must protect Yvonne from the
demonic forces that are trying to capture her
and claim her for his own.

CLAIMED BY A VAMPIRE

Available in February wherever books are sold.

HARLEQUIN® HISTORICAL:
Where love is timeless

INTRODUCING
LOUISE ALLEN'S
MOST SCANDALOUS TRILOGY YET!

Danger & Desire

Leaving the sultry shores of India behind them, the passengers of the *Bengal Queen* face a new life ahead in England—until a shipwreck throws their plans into disarray….

Can Alistair and Perdita's illicit onboard flirtation survive the glittering social whirl of London?

Washed up on an island populated by ruffians, virginal Averil must rely on rebel captain Luc for protection….

And honorable Callum finds himself falling for his brother's fiancée!

Take the plunge this February!

Ravished by the Rake
February 2012

Seduced by the Scoundrel
March 2012

Married to a Stranger
April 2012